"So whoever wins the science fair gets the cash prize," Ray Roches said, leaning against his locker. "Plus the loser has to be the other person's servant for a whole day. That means, you *buy my barbecued chips*. And you *do my homework*."

Ray was crazy to think *I'd* be bringing *him* chips! Please! The other way around was more like it. "Okay, sure," I said, taking off my sneakers and socks. "I'll make that bet. I mean, hey, it's your funeral."

"Wrong!" Ray shoved me hard. "It's yours!"

I went sprawling backward, sliding on the slippery tile floor of the boys' locker room. "No!" I cried. "Stop!" I was heading right toward the Patch!

I tried grabbing onto a locker door handle, but it came off in my hand. I kept skidding on my heels, like a car on ice out of control.

All of a sudden my feet landed in this sticky, gooey, fuzzy area. I couldn't move! It was the Patch!

Within seconds, crusty yellow-green stuff started popping up all over my feet! I was growing white fuzzballs between my toes faster than Ray could remember his locker combination!

"I'll get you for this!" I yelled.

Get ready to be grossed out with more

SLIMEBALLS:

#2 FUN GUS SLIMES THE BUS!

#3 THE SLITHERS BUY A BOA

SLIMEBALLS

FUN GUS & POLLY PUS

Bullseye Books

Random House 🏠 New York

CHAPTER ONE

"Good boy. Nice job. Keep it up." I ran my fingers over the slimy, wet surface of my new fungus, *Moldus Maximus*. It had tiny bumps, sort of like pimples.

"Guuuuuuus!" My mother barged into the garage, shrieking my name. As if I wouldn't hear her! She has this really high-pitched voice—she sings in a choir at church, and she can really belt it out when she wants to. "Guuuuuuus!"

"Yeah, Mom?" I said. "I'm right here—you don't have to yell."

"What are you *doing?*" my mother asked. "Get your hand off that—that thing! It looks like a tongue!"

"It's not a tongue, Mom, it's a fungus," I told her. "They like to be touched. If you pay attention to them, they'll grow faster."

"And you...let me get this straight...you *want*

them to grow?" She looked around at my collection of molds, horrified.

She wanted them all to die. I knew that.

But they weren't going to. I owned a ton of them. And my fungi were going to thrive!

Moldus Maximus was the cream of the crop, a very rare *Fistulina Hepatica*. The top fuzz of the fungi. The common name of my current fungal favorite was Beefsteak Polypore. I found it on a dead log, behind our house.

Basically it looks like a giant red tongue, and it drips this liquid that looks like real blood. It's the coolest kind of polypore fungus there is.

I have a huge collection of moldy food and fungi in my garage. That's where my mom made me go after she found out I'd turned the vegetable bin in the fridge into Mold Central. She was always complaining about how the mushrooms went bad.

That's where my mom and I disagree. To her, mushrooms go *bad* when they become brown and slimy and furry. But to me, they're just getting *good*. It's like the starting point. Before that, they're just wasting my time. As if I want to eat them in a salad. Please. They're valuable research tools, not a meal.

I have all my molds arranged according to size and color. It really makes an attractive display. Each one is special in its own way—maybe it's the color, or the stench, or the fact it came from our refrigerator. Whatever. All molds are welcome in my lab.

"Well, it's time to stop...with that—that—tongue thing, and come into the house for breakfast." She took a few steps across the garage. She doesn't come much closer than that to my lab. She doesn't even park her car in here anymore. She's afraid. As if a mold is going to jump up and bite her. That doesn't happen, except in the movies. The really *cool* movies.

"I already had breakfast," I told her.

"You didn't"—she looked nervously at the rows of fungus around us, in various stages of growth—"tell me you didn't...eat one of those..."

"Mom, I've told you a hundred times," I said. "I don't eat my experiments. I had a bowl of cereal when I got up, okay? It was a little stale, definitely, but not moldy." It was a shame, really. There is this entire food group that just doesn't decompose. I guess it's all the preservatives.

And what about all the stuff that comes in cans? "Nonperishable" means it'll never go bad. What's the fun in that?

Maybe cereal won't rot, but at least milk can go sour. Not that my mom will let it. She tosses everything out about a month before the expiration date.

"Well, if you aren't going to have any more breakfast, then you might as well head off to school," my mother said. "Jake's leaving soon."

Jake is my older brother. *Jerk* is more like it. He's a junior in high school, which makes him about five years older than me. And he never lets me forget it. He's a hot-shot football player, and the star of the basketball team, and last spring he was rated the best pitcher in the whole state. I'd like to pitch *him*.

Jake's constantly telling me what a loser I am, just because I don't play three sports. Or one, for that matter. But I think *he's* the loser—he can't even pass the easiest biology class there is!

"I can walk to school by myself, Mom," I said. "I don't need Jake to hold my hand when I cross the street."

"Well, all right, but I'd prefer that you went together," my mother said. "At least come into the house and get your books and lunch!"

"No problem," I said. The most important thing I had to remember was my *lunch*. Our school cafeteria is the worst in the entire world.

"Well, Gus? Are you coming or not?" My mother was standing by the garage door.

"Just a sec, Mom—I want to show you my experiment for the science fair," I said. "Come here for a second."

"Well, er, I have to get going or I'll be late for work," my mom said, her nose wrinkling up like a prune.

"Mom, it'll only take a second. This is really cool!" I said. "I'm going to win first prize at

4

the science fair this year."

"You are?" my mother asked, edging a few steps closer. She sounded proud.

I nodded. "Sure. Check out *Moldus Maximus!*"

"Looks very...um...nice," she said, practically choking out the words. "Considering it looks like a...slimy tongue, I guess." She wouldn't even look me in the eye.

Parents. They're always telling you to achieve. But do they want to see the results? No.

"Mom, you can't appreciate it from way over there," I said. "Come on! Smell it! Touch it!" I held the fungus toward my mother. She looked as if she was about to lose it.

"You know, Gus," she said, stepping back. "Whatever happened to playing video games? You used to love those!"

"You made me stop, remember? You told me I was addicted!"

"Oh. Right. Well, couldn't you give up growing mold and start doing something else? What about playing baseball—or football? Like Jake! I'm sure he'd be happy to teach you all he knows and—"

"I don't want to be Jake junior," I said.

"But why not?" my mother cried. "He's got everything going for him. He's the star athlete for the Spartans, and he's on the student council, and he—"

"Talking about me again?" Jake walked into

the garage, grinning from ear to ear. "Well, what can I say? It's all true. I *am* a star."

I rolled my eyes. "Give me a break," I muttered. Talk about a big ego!

"Hey, Shrimp. Here's your lunch. Catch!" Jake threw my lunch bag across the garage like a football.

I tried to grab it, but the bag crashed right into my dish of rotting chocolate pudding, knocking it onto the garage floor.

"Aaaah!" My mother held her arms in front of her, shielding herself from the stinky, slimy brownish green goo.

"Hey, cool! I killed the pudding!" Jake crowed. "This is like Shoot the Duck at the state fair!"

I frowned at him. "Did you have to knock that one over? I've had him since January!"

"Peuw...it smells like it!" Jake held his nose. "Come on, Shrimp. We're going to be late."

I gave *Moldus Maximus* one last rub for good luck before I left. My hand smelled kind of funny after I touched the mold. But I figured nothing stank worse than Ray Roches, who sits behind me at school.

Ray's the most obnoxious kid in our entire class. I was planning on leaving a small piece of my prize fungus in his desk after the science fair. Maybe he'd transfer to another class!

"I'm sick of walking to school," Jake complained as we trudged across the park. "But in a couple more days, I won't have to!"

"Because you're going to do all the teachers a favor—and drop out?" I clasped my hands together. "Oh, Jake, I'm so proud!"

"Shut up. I'm not dropping out, loser. I'm getting my own car. Mom and Dad said we're going to pick one out this weekend!" Jake was tossing a football up into the air and catching it again as he walked. Show-off.

"Well, get a big one," I said. "You know, a van. You can use it to move away from home."

"What makes you think I'm going to move?" Jake asked. "I've already decided I'm going to the U. right here in Thornhill. They're giving me a scholarship, remember?"

Scholarship? Try jockship! Or maybe *sinking* ship. I bet my brother couldn't even spell the word *scholarship*, much less get one. "Yeah, well, they could always change their *minds*."

"Dude." Jake laughed. "As if they'd turn away the best high school athlete in the state!" He bent over, holding his stomach, as if it was the funniest thing he'd ever heard. Lucky for my brother, a sense of humor wasn't required for admittance to the college.

"Hey, Shrimp—go out for a pass!" Jake pump-faked the football a couple of times.

I sighed. Every day, it was the same. Catch your lunch. Go out for a pass. The Jerk *never*

asked whether I *wanted* to catch his stupid football!

I ran ahead, crossing the large, open section of the park. I figured the faster I ran, the farther away I'd get—then, when I finally turned around, there was no way Jake would ever be able to throw the ball to me. I mean, he has a good arm and all, but 100 yards?

I turned around to see how far away Jake was. The sun was in my eyes, and I couldn't see a thing. Dots were swimming in front of me.

All of a sudden, this shadow fell over my face, getting bigger and bigger....

It was the football! It clocked me right on the head!

I crashed to the ground, crunching some twigs underneath me, my face pressed against a clump of mud.

All I could hear was Jake, cackling with laughter.

"Bro, you all right?" he called to me. "Dude, I really hit you with that pass, didn't I? Hit you—get it?"

"Ha ha," I muttered, my mouth full of grass. I spit out a wet green wad. "Very funny."

That's when I saw it. The mushroom I'd been dreaming about. The most perfect, slimiest, stinkiest mushroom in the world. It was shaped funny, as if it had gotten mixed up with a dandelion—

It was all frayed around the edges and had this dingy yellowish tinge. I plucked it out of the ground and stood up, holding it in front of my face to examine it more closely.

"What are you doing?" Jake asked, jogging over to me. "Did you find some money—Oh. Eeuuw. Disgusting. Put that thing down."

"It's so cool!" I said, excited.

"Gus, you're a *freak*," Jake said. His lip was curled up in a sneer. "What are you doing even touching that thing?"

"What do you mean? This is the most major mushroom discovery I've ever made! This kind of fungus could make me famous!" I cried. I'd never seen anything like it, not in any of my guidebooks. It must be a new strain!

"Yeah. You'll be famous, all right. For being a total weirdo," Jake said. "Man, why couldn't I have a *normal* brother? I mean, is that so much to ask? Just once, I want to throw the football and actually have someone catch it, instead of stopping to pick up some mutant plant and—"

I'd had enough. Jake was always going on about how he wanted a wide receiver for a little brother. I was sick of it!

And I knew just how to get him back for hitting me on the head with the football. Having that mushroom slime him would ruin his day. If I threw it at him and hit him on the nose, the way he'd clocked me with the football, he'd throw a fit. That was something I couldn't wait to see. Mr. Big Shot showing up at high school with slime on his nose.

While he kept talking, I grabbed the mushroom stem—and hurled it right at his face!

The mushroom went right into his mouth—a direct hit!

Jake's face turned half-red and half-green. He made a gagging, gasping noise and started staggering around the field.

My brother couldn't breathe!

CHAPTER TWO

Jake hit the ground butt first.

I couldn't have been happier.

But then I realized I was going to lose the mushroom. Once it went into Jake's stomach, both he *and* the mushroom would be history. I couldn't let that happen!

"No! Jake! Don't eat it!" I shouted, leaping on top of him.

Jake coughed, then pulled the mushroom out of his mouth. "Why? Is it poisonous?"

"No! Well, sure, probably it's very poisonous," I told him. "Most of them are. But that's not the point."

"It isn't? I could have died!" Jake wailed. He was pitiful!

"No. See, the point is, I want this for my fungal collection." I picked up the saliva-covered mushroom and put it in my pocket.

11

"Fungus freak," my brother muttered, shaking his head as he stood up and started walking toward school.

"Football freak!" I cried, running past him toward my middle school. I didn't want to be seen with a loser like my brother!

Besides, I couldn't wait to sign up for the science fair. I was going to show off *Moldus Maximus* to the world!

"People, settle down!" Mr. Starchfield said as he walked into our classroom. "Take your seats! Let's get learning!"

Nobody moved. He says the same thing every day. What else would we be doing? Mr. Starchfield's an okay teacher, but he kind of grates on my nerves. He's into the "positive thinking" approach, which basically means he walks around all day spouting stupid sayings. Sometimes Mr. Starchfield acts almost as stupid as Ray.

Ray's the biggest guy in the seventh grade, and he's never liked me, or me him. He's tall and strong, and when he shakes my chair from behind, it's like being inside a popcorn popper. I hate it when he does that. And his hair is cut really short. I figure he must get his crew cut re-cut every other day. I call him "Baldy" and "Roach." He calls me "Moldy" and "Goose." We're really close.

Ray's a total pig sometimes. He has this really

disgusting habit of eating barbecued potato chips for breakfast every morning.

Of course, I can't blame Ray for bringing his own food. A bunch of kids nearly died once after the "All You Can Eat" Friday Fish Fry in the cafeteria. The fish turned out to be from the Parasite River. It's really the Paradise River, but we all call it the Parasite, because it's full of festering junk.

At my school, if you don't bring your lunch, you're crazy—or sick. Like, every day, at around two o'clock. Puke City. You can tell the kids who eat at the cafeteria because after lunch they have to jump up and run out of the room during class. I just sit there and pray they'll make it in time. The last thing I want is some kid barfing on me because he's too dumb to bring his lunch. Get a clue, I want to say. Or at least get one of those vomit bags they give you on airplanes!

Ray waved a giant chip in the air, then shoved it into his mouth. When he bit down, chip pieces crumbled down onto his shirt and his desk. But Ray didn't care. He just shoved another chip into his mouth and crunched it. "You're late, Goose," he said. "I thought nerds like you were never late."

"Yeah, well, I thought blockheads like you were never on time," I said, sliding into my chair. "What happened? Did you finally figure out how to set your alarm clock?"

Ray looked confused for a second. "No! I figured that out last year."

"Congratulations," I said. "Anyway, I was working on something very important, and *that's* why I was late. You'll find out all about it soon enough."

Ray tapped a barbecued chip against his chin. "Something important to a nerd...what could that be...I know! You were trying to make sure your pants were short enough! Nice high waters, by the way!"

I shook my head. "They're shorts, okay?"

He polished off the giant bag of barbecued chips, then downed his huge soda in one gulp. Then he let out a big belch. Mr. Starchfield gave Ray a horrified look, then started class.

"Good morning, everybody." Mr. Starchfield forced a smile. "Thank you, Ray." He cleared his throat, looking totally disgusted.

"No problem," Ray said. "The belch is mightier than the bell, right?" He laughed at his own joke.

"You're disgusting," Polly Petri called out from across the room.

I turned around to look at Ray. "Get some mouthwash, will you? Some of us are trying to *breathe* in here."

"I didn't know geeks needed oxygen," Ray shot back. "Don't you just breathe through your gills, Goose?"

14

"For your information, a goose—which I am not—is a bird, not a *fish*." I shook my head. "Idiot." How did he avoid getting left back *year* after *year*?

"Ahem. People! I have an important announcement to make," Mr. Starchfield said. He straightened his bow tie and put on his reading glasses, peering at a sheet of paper. "As you all know, today is the day that you'll be signing up for the science fair."

There were a couple of snickers. Most kids didn't plan on entering the fair. Hey, I didn't care. It was just going to be that much easier to win.

"Your projects will be due at the end of next week. That gives you two weeks to work on them, if you haven't already started. I encourage all of you to take part. After all, it's more fun to participate than it is to spectate! Right, kids?" Mr. Starchfield pushed his glasses up on the bridge of his nose and peered at us. "So, I have the sign-up sheet right here. Who wants to put their name down?"

I raised my hand.

"That's the spirit, Gus. Come right up," Mr. Starchfield said.

I stood up and started walking toward his desk, where the clipboard was resting on the edge. I was halfway there when Mr. Starchfield slapped his forehead. "My goodness gracious!

How could I have forgotten to mention the most important thing? There's a prize this year!"

"Does the winner of the science fair get the dweeb of the year award?" Ray asked with a laugh. "Way to go, Moulder!"

I turned around, sticking out my tongue at him. "Moron!"

Mr. Starchfield gave both of us a disapproving glance. "As I was saying, boys, this year's science fair is being sponsored by Buster Dexter, Thornhill Middle School's greatest scientist ever! Mr. Dexter has graciously offered to donate a one-hundred-dollar prize to the winning—"

Mr. Starchfield hadn't even finished his sentence when everyone in the classroom leaped out of their seats. I was shoved up against the blackboard—practically trampled—while everyone got into line to sign up!

"Hey, watch it!" I cried, my ribs almost crushed.

"You must have known about the prize," Polly Petri said, standing in front of me. "How did you find out so fast?"

"Because that nerd, Buster Dexter, is like his great-grandfather or something," Ray sneered. "They have the same nerd gene."

"It's called gene-*ius*," I said.

"We'll see," Ray nodded. "Now that you're actually going to have some competition this year, you might not win, geekbrain."

"Oh, right," I said. "I guess you're going to beat me?" Right. As if. The last time Ray passed science without summer school was when we had to color in the right colors for different animals. Even then, he made the elephant blue.

"Please put a brief description of your project next to your name," Mr. Starchfield said. "No shoving! No pushing! When you wait your turn, you get your turn!"

"Yeah, sure," Ray muttered, pushing in front of me.

Polly slipped past Ray and ended up in front of *him*.

It's dog-eat-dog in my class—but I told myself to just relax. It didn't matter how many people signed up in front of me, or whether my name was first or last on the list. I was still going to win.

I craned my neck, trying to get a look at the list.

"*That's* what you're entering in the science fair?" I asked when Polly wrote down "Display of Planets Rotating Around the Sun."

She turned around, flipping her long, poufed brown hair over her shoulder. "Sure, why not?"

"Like we haven't seen that a million times before," I said, folding my arms across my chest.

"Mine's going to be *better,* okay?" Polly said in a huff. Just because she's pretty, and a cheerleader, she thinks she's better than everyone else. "Why are you even *talking* to me?"

17

Well, Polly, I wanted to say, don't get your hopes up about winning—not with me around! Why do some people think they can do science projects once a year and actually be good at them? For me, it was a lifelong devotion. Kind of the way Polly felt about her hair.

She went back to her desk, and Ray stepped to the front of the line. I moved over so that I could see what he wrote.

He tapped the pencil against his chin and stared at the ceiling tiles, as if he were thinking about entering them in the science fair. Not that it wouldn't be a good project. You could test the acoustics, or the material they're made out of. But knowing Ray, he'd probably just count the holes in them.

"Well, Ray?" Mr. Starchfield prompted. "What's your project? We need to get going with today's assignments, so, if you don't mind..."

"Just a second. I'm thinking," Ray said.

"Better make it an hour, Mr. Starchfield," I said.

Suddenly, Ray leaned over to write down his project idea. "To Be Announced," he wrote in giant letters.

Mr. Starchfield cleared his throat. "Well, you'll have to let me know tomorrow. That's the deadline."

"Oh, sure. No problem. I just have to check on some stuff at home," Ray said.

"You mean…cheat?" I asked.

"No, *moldface*. We have this vegetable garden, and I have to pick out something to grow," Ray said.

"Vegetables don't *grow* in two weeks," I pointed out.

Ray gave me a superior smile. "Mine will."

"What are you going to do? Threaten them? Stare at them and say, 'Grow, peas, or else!'" I laughed. As if that would work!

"Gus, I believe you're last," Mr. Starchfield said, handing me the pencil.

"Yeah, and get used to it!" Ray said.

"I might be the last one to sign up, but *you're* going to be last in the fair," I replied.

"Gus Moulder," I wrote. "Project: *Moldus Maximus.*"

It was so cool-sounding. I ought to win just because of the name!

Some students had written down "Explore Various Colors of Kool-Aid," "The Metric System Is for Me," or "Volcano!"

Please. I was doing volcanoes in kindergarten. That's why they kicked me out. My volcano erupted in the middle of "sleepytime," spewing lava all over everyone's nap mats. It was totally awesome.

"Hey, Goose," Ray said, tapping me on the shoulder after I sat back down in my seat. "What's your project?"

"None of your business," I muttered through clenched teeth.

"Is too," Ray argued. "I told you about mine!"

I turned around, one eyebrow raised. "'To be announced' doesn't really tell me anything. I mean, it is a little *vague*."

"So? I told you about the garden. Come on. I gotta know now, if I want to beat you. What's your plan?"

"My plan is to win," I said smugly.

"Well, we'll see about that," Ray said.

"Oh, yeah?" I replied.

"Yeah!" Ray stood up and started shaking my desk chair, the way he always does.

"Quit it!" I yelled, jumping up.

"Tell me about your project, and I will!" he said, still shaking my chair.

"Hey, stupid, I'm over *here*," I told him.

"All right, Ray and Gus! That's enough!" Mr. Starchfield said, clapping his hands.

"Thank you, thank you." Ray took a bow, and everyone started laughing.

"Very funny. Boys, I think you've disrupted class enough!" Mr. Starchfield said. "I want to see both of you, right here, after school, for detention. You can make up some of the precious time we've already lost!"

Ray slunk back into his seat behind me with a groan.

"But I didn't do anything!" I protested. "And I

can't stay after school," I said. "I have to get home and—"

I was about to say, "look after my mold," when I realized I couldn't say anything about it. I didn't want Ray to copy my idea. He's been trying to copy my homework for the past five years!

"Gus has to get home right away and take a nap," Ray said. "Being so smart is hard on his little brain. Isn't it, Gus?"

"Like you'd know," I said. "And I don't take naps. I don't sleep through *class*, either—not like *some* people!" I said, looking in Ray's direction.

"Can I help it if I need my sleep?" Ray asked.

"Yeah, your beauty sleep," I said. "Well, guess what. It's not working!"

"Gus, settle down. Stop provoking him! Ray, why don't you have another chip or two," Mr. Starchfield said. "Perhaps that will keep your mouth occupied long enough to stop talking!"

"Cool!" Ray opened his desk and pulled out a fresh bag of barbecued chips. I think he has a lifetime supply in there.

I got out my book report. But I couldn't concentrate. I was going to win a hundred dollars for my mold!

No matter what Ray did to try and stop me.

CHAPTER THREE

Ray and I were walking into the locker room after gym class later that morning. Ray was trudging behind me—as if he's permanently got to be looking at the back of my head or something.

I hate P.E. Coach K., the football coach, is our teacher. He's incredibly tough. He's always making us do push-ups, pull-ups, and sit-ups. Basically, we do anything that involves the word "up," including throw up when he makes us work too hard.

Coach K. coached my brother Jake five years ago, so he's always saying stuff like "Moulder, I remember your brother...Now, that was a kid with a good arm," or "You oughta take a coupla lessons from Jake!" or "Are you sure you're *related* to Jake?" Being a younger brother is the pits.

Ray jabbed me in the arm, in the same spot where he'd spiked the volleyball onto me. "Hey. The winner of the science fair gets a hundred bucks this year."

Duh, I thought. I mean, hadn't we been sitting in the same room when Mr. Starchfield told us that? "And? What's your point, Einstein?" I asked.

"Well. My point is that I'm going to get that money. So don't even think about beating me," Ray said.

"Or?" I asked.

"Or—or—" Ray stammered. I guess he hadn't had enough time to figure out that part.

"Look, Ray," I said, putting my hand on his shoulder. "I don't want to sound mean, but come on. Your chances of winning the science fair are about as good as my chances of being picked first for softball during recess. Plain and simple? It's not going to happen."

"You think you're so smart." Ray glared at me, his eyebrows crunched together.

"Well, it's not really a question of *thinking* I'm smart," I said. "It's actually something I know."

"Hrrmph," Ray grunted, tossing my hand off his shoulder. He looked like a cat getting ready to pounce. If he'd had a tail, it would have been swishing back and forth. "Okay, Goose. I didn't want to do this, but I have no choice."

"To do what?" I asked. "Are you going to give

up? Are you going to cross your name off the list?"

"No, stupid. There's only one thing to do now," Ray went on, pushing me backward by poking his finger into my chest.

I ignored him and turned away. I put my foot on the bench and started taking off my sneakers and socks. "What are you going to do? Transfer to another school where they only require gym and they never have science fairs?"

"No, doofus." Ray snapped a towel in the air. "We have to make a bet."

"A *bet?*" I repeated. "Why?"

"So that whoever wins the science fair gets the cash prize. *Plus* the loser—that would be *you*—has to do something really embarrassing in front of the whole school," Ray declared.

"Well, uh..." I laughed, tossing my dirty socks into my locker. "Isn't losing the science fair going to be embarrassing enough for you?" I asked.

"Embarrassing for *you*, you mean," Ray said. "Especially since you're so smart and all. When I win, everyone's going to wonder what happened."

"I'll say," I muttered under my breath.

"And then, to make it even *more* humiliating, whoever loses has to be the other person's servant for a whole day. That means you buy my chips. You do my homework. I'll be king for a day."

Yeah, right, I thought. King of idiots!

24

Ray rubbed his hands together, and some barbecued crumbs fell to the floor, even though he hadn't eaten any chips for hours.

Ray was crazy to think that I'd be bringing *him* chips! Please! The other way around was more like it. "Okay, sure," I said. "I'll make that bet. I mean, hey, it's your funeral."

"Wrong!" Ray shoved me harder. "I think it's yours!"

I went sprawling backward, sliding on the slippery tile floor. "No!" I cried. "Stop!" I was heading right toward the Patch!

I tried grabbing onto a locker door handle, but it came off in my hand. I kept skidding on my heels, out of control, like a car on ice.

If I didn't stop, I was going to hurtle into the germ zone—toes first! Nobody came out of there without athlete's foot and toenail fungus. Nobody!

When Jake was in middle school, there was this amazing wide receiver on the football team...*until* he landed in the Patch. The guy never caught a pass again. He couldn't run because his toenails were full of junk, and he had to stop every five yards to scratch his feet!

I felt as if I was moving in slow motion. All of a sudden my feet landed in this sticky, gooey, fuzzy area. I couldn't move! It was the Patch!

"Ray! Help me!" I screamed.

"What's up, Goose?" he asked.

"I'm in the Patch! I'm stuck! Help me out!" I pleaded.

"Oh, no," Ray said. "Look, dude, I didn't mean to do that! Sorry! Here, let me get you a towel, okay?" He tossed a white towel toward me.

I caught it and quickly started drying off one foot. Then I leaped out of the Patch, my other foot coming free with an oozing, sucking noise. I furiously tried to rub that foot dry, too, hoping I'd get rid of the fungus before it got rid of me.

But there was a problem—the towel was about as damp as Ray's armpits. And almost as stinky! The towel didn't do anything but smear the fungus all over my feet!

"Hey, Ray! What's with this towel?" I squeezed one end of it, and water dripped onto the floor underneath the bench.

"Oh, *that* towel. Whoops! Guess I must have handed you the wrong one!" Ray said.

"What do you mean the *wrong one*?" I asked.

"Well, I thought I was throwing you a fresh, clean towel," Ray said. He waved another white towel in the air. "But that's this one, right here! Which means...oh, Gus. You're not going to like this."

"Like what?" I asked.

"Well, it's about the towel. See, the floor was wet in here when I showed up for class. And I almost wiped out! I'm telling you, it was dangerous. So I took this towel and I mopped up the junk—oh, right about over there, I guess." Ray pointed to the Patch. "And, oh, gee, gosh, golly, Gus. It must have the funky fungus stuff on it, too!"

"Roches! You dimwit!" I yelled, throwing the fungus-filled towel back at him.

He laughed, snorting through his nose, as he ducked to avoid the infected towel. "Oh, yeah. *I'm* the dimwit. Then how come I'm not the one with green stuff growing between my toes!"

I glanced down at my poor bare feet. He was right. Within seconds, crusty yellow-green stuff started popping up all over my feet! I was growing white fuzzballs between my toes faster than Ray could remember his locker combination!

"I'll get you for this, Roach!" I yelled.

"Oh, right. I'm *so* scared!" he said, still cackling.

I jumped up and ran out of the locker room. I tore down the hall at top speed toward the nurse's office.

Usually I had to be dragged there, because Nurse Gillette is the weirdest R.N. on the planet. But this was an emergency! I needed help—now!

The last time I saw Nurse Gillette, she shoved the tongue depressor thing so far down in my mouth that I actually gagged. I spewed all over her precious white uniform. You'd think that might make her change the way she does things, but no. Now she wears this pink plastic baby's bib when she checks kids' tonsils.

I took a deep breath and knocked on the door. "Nurse Gillette?"

"Come in!" came a scratchy voice.

I pushed the door open slowly. "I need your help."

"Who doesn't?" Nurse Gillette was sitting at her desk, with her huge platform nurse's shoes propped on top of it. She's tall enough without the platforms, but I guess she likes to tower over everyone. She swung her legs off the desk. "What seems to be the problem, Mr. Mold?"

"That's Moulder," I said. "Gus Moulder."

She opened her file cabinet and started flipping through it. "Aha!" She yanked out a bright red file. "Augustus Moulder."

Augustus. Did she have to remind me?

She opened the file on her desk and shuffled through a bunch of papers. "Let's see...the patient has a history of sudden, unexplainable nausea...and a mole on his right ankle. Correct?"

I held up my ankle in front of her face. "That's why I'm here, actually."

"Oh—you want me to burn the mole off?" Nurse Gillette reached for a bottle of acid.

"No!" I cried. "Not my ankle, Nurse Gillette! It's my feet."

"Foot, ankle, same difference." She patted the

table, which was covered with white paper. "Hop up and let me have a look."

"Okay, but put down the acid first," I said.

"Boy, you're as chicken as the men in the 72nd Unit, Private Moulder," she said. Nurse Gillette used to be in the Army or Navy or something, but the rumor around school is that she got kicked out. She probably wiped out the entire unit. It wouldn't surprise me. "All right, now, tell me what the problem is," she said, once I was seated on the table. "And don't leave out any important details!"

"I-I was in the boys' locker room, after gym class," I said.

"Be more specific," she said.

"It was about...three minutes ago?" I guessed.

She jotted something on my chart. "Proceed."

"Well, uh, Ray Roches—you know him?" I asked.

"Know him!" Nurse Gillette exclaimed. "He's the best patient I've ever had."

"Really?" I asked. "What did you treat him for?"

"That's confidential information," Nurse Gillette said. "But let's just say it was a matter of built-up stomach acid. I mean, it could have been. Never you mind. Continue, please."

"Ray shoved me, and I got toenail fungus from the zone," I said. "You know, the Patch. The worst place in the world to go to, and I was there!"

She peered at me. "Son, have you ever been treated for your paranoia?"

"Huh?" I asked.

"Paranoia. Being afraid of stuff for no reason," she explained. "You were in the locker room. So are hundreds of boys, every day. And how many of them get toenail fungus?"

I shrugged. "About half of them?"

"Right," Nurse Gillette said. "So the chances of you getting it are very slim."

"1 in 2? That's slim?" I asked. Nurse Gillette sure has a weird way of looking at things.

"But, let's examine the affected area, just to make sure," she said. She took out her little pencil-shaped light and shined it on my feet. Her eyes grew wide. "Well, well. Looks like we got ourselves some creepy critters. But we'll take care of them in no time."

"Phew," I sighed.

"Don't worry, Augustus. Nature gave us a cure for this one," Nurse Gillette said.

She sounded almost reassuring, for once in her life. I felt my shoulders relax, and I smiled. "Nature's cure, huh? What's that? Herbs or something?"

"Iodine." Nurse Gillette held up a bucket of the stuff and plunged my feet right into it.

"B-b-b-b-b-b-blisters!" I screamed. "I've got blisters!" I'd been wearing a new pair of sneakers for the past few days, and they'd rubbed half the skin off my heels.

The iodine seeped into my cuts. My feet felt as if they were on fire!

I started hopping around her office, my feet stuck in the bucket.

Nurse Gillette just stood there, nodding. "Swish it around, that's right, just like at the dentist!" She reached out and held my arm. "Just a few minutes more, and the fungus will be dead!"

And so will I! I thought.

Suddenly the bell rang. Nurse Gillette let go of me, as if she was in a trance.

This was my chance to escape!

I pulled the bucket off my feet and ran out into the hallway. My feet were stained bright pink, and they throbbed all over. I was yelling with pain as the iodine dried in my heel blisters.

Everyone was changing rooms between classes. But nobody even blinked when they saw me running away, screaming. That's the way *everyone* acts when they come out of Nurse Gillette's office.

You were lucky to get away with your life!

But the battle had only just begun.

The toenail fungus felt as if it was eating me alive—from the bottom up!

CHAPTER FOUR

"What does athlete's foot feel like?" I rubbed my toes against the floor as I gulped my OJ the next morning. Right from the carton—just the way I like it!

"Don't worry, Shrimp. You'll never get it in a million years," Jake said. "You're not an athlete, remember?"

"You don't have to be an athlete to get athlete's foot," I said. "Just like you don't have to be a *scholar* to get a scholarship." I looked at him and grinned. Top that, I thought.

"Well, what are your symptoms?" Jake asked cheerfully. That's how dumb he is. He didn't even get that I was making a dig at him.

"First of all, you should know something," I said. "Yesterday in gym class? I stepped in the Patch."

Jake dropped his spoon. "Dude! Not the

Patch! Haven't I told you a million times never to—"

"I know, I know. But...well, it was an accident," I said. Telling Jake I got shoved into the Patch would only make things worse. He'd never stop teasing me. "Anyway, I cleaned my feet a thousand times yesterday. But they itch all the time. And they're kind of this green color, you know, like the way an orange looks if you leave it in your locker too long?"

"With that white fuzz all around the edges?" Jake asked, sitting up in his chair. "Do your feet smell? I mean—more than usual?"

"Yeah. And there are these weird things in between my toes that kind of look like miniature cotton balls," I said. "And when you take them off, new ones grow back, like, instantly!"

"Cool!" Jake said.

"Boys! Do you have to talk about these things while we eat?" my mother complained, putting a bowl of gray oatmeal on the table in front of us.

"I've never had that, but I did have this weird infection on my leg once. It looks kind of like this, actually." Jake pulled a strip of orange peel out of the marmalade jar. "All stringy, and kind of orange, and—"

"Jake! You're supposed to be setting an example, not encouraging him," my father said, putting down the newspaper. "Really, now."

Just when my brother was starting to act cool. Parents ruin everything.

"Gus, if you picked up something from school, why don't you ask the nurse about it?" my mother suggested.

"I did, Mom. She almost killed me," I explained.

"Now, now, exaggerating never helped any-thing," my father said sternly.

"I've got some spray you can use," Jake said. "It's in a can upstairs. Put some on your feet before you go to school and I swear that crawling crud will be cleared up before lunch."

"Really?" I asked.

"Sure thing," Jake said.

I couldn't believe it. My brother was actually being helpful, for once. Maybe he wasn't such a creep after all.

"Jake, there are some big car sales this week-end," my father announced, pushing the newspa-per across the table to him. "I think we'll be able to get a good deal on a car for you."

"Do you think I should get a two-door or a four-door?" Jake asked. "Or a moon roof or a sun roof—"

I yawned, pushing my chair back from the table. "See ya!" I said. Not that I don't like cars! But I had more important things to do.

I ran upstairs to Jake's room. There were a couple of cans of stuff on his dresser, but I grabbed the one that said, CURES FOOT FUNGUS INSTANTLY.

I took off my new sneakers and socks and sprayed my feet for about five minutes, until it was so foggy that I couldn't see across the room. The spray must have worked, because my feet stopped itching instantly. Then I put my socks and sneakers on and ran back downstairs.

I went out toward the garage. I whistled as I put my key in the lock. Things were beginning to look up. The Patch wasn't going to be fatal, thanks to Jake. The science fair was coming up in two weeks, and as soon as I won, I'd have a hundred dollars, and Ray would be my slave. There was no doubt about it. My life was definitely on an upswing.

I pulled the door open and strode over to the ledge underneath the window. "Good morning, little *Russula fragrantissima,*" I said, checking out a small specimen I'd gathered a couple of days before. "Hello, macaroni and cheese." Was I glad we'd had it for dinner last July—it smelled great!

I reached up to pet *Moldus Maximus.* My hand felt something horrible, something scary and terrifying—

It felt nothing at all! *Moldus Maximus* was gone!

I searched the entire garage. Don't panic, I told myself. My heart was pounding in my chest. *Moldus Maximus*—gone! How? I stared at the garage floor, then got down and crawled around on my hands and knees. Maybe it fell on the floor!

"Maxi!" I called, searching in every cob-webbed corner of the garage. "Come back!"

But there was no trail of slime—no evidence that it had moved on its own. That could only mean one thing. Someone *else* had taken it. But who?

My mom—who was so sick of all my molds taking up so much room in the garage that she now parked in the street? But that didn't make sense. She would have gotten rid of all my molds, not just *Moldus Maximus*.

My dad, who thought I ought to take up a "real hobby," like a butterfly collection?

Jake? Would he destroy my favorite mold, just because I couldn't catch a football?

I stared at the floor again, looking for foot-prints, animal tracks, any sign of foul play.

That's when I saw it. A trail of chips. Orange chips!

"Ray Roches!" I cried. "Sabotage!"

CHAPTER FIVE

"All right, Ray. Where is it?" I stood behind Ray's desk and shook his chair, using his scare tactics on him. I was desperate. "Hand it over."

"What are you talking about?" Ray took an extra-large barbecued chip and shoved it into his mouth.

"You know what I'm talking about," I said, shaking the chair again.

"Mmrnsphgyf," Ray said with a casual shrug. I think he said, "No, I don't." Or else he was choking on the chip.

"Yes, you do," I said. "You stole my experiment for the science fair. I don't know how you did it, but—" I started tapping my foot against the floor. Just a little bit, to make my point.

But then I started tapping it even harder. And then I was pounding both feet against the floor. Pretty soon they were twitching out of control!

Forget Ray! Forget Maxi! My feet were itching like crazy!

"Is that some new dance?" Ray asked with a guffaw. "The Nerd Special?"

I couldn't stop moving my feet! They were twitching back and forth, as if they had a mind of their own. I reached down to scratch them, but I couldn't get to the part that itched the most, so I yanked off my sneakers and then my socks.

"Whoa!" Ray cried. "Creature from the green lagoon!"

I looked down at my feet. They were covered with gooey green junk and thick white bumps!

"Aieee!"

"Put your shoes back on!"

"What's *wrong* with you?"

"Weirdo!"

Here I was, infected with a deadly strain of foot fungus, and all my classmates were pressed against the blackboard, scared to death of me! Some friends!

I hopped back and forth from one foot to the other in total agony. If I kept moving, it didn't itch as much. "What's the matter? Haven't you ever seen anyone with athlete's foot before?" I asked.

"Yeah, sure," Ray said. "And it didn't look like that!"

"Yeah, that's gross," Polly added. "Maybe you should stay home for a while."

"Oh, you'd love that, wouldn't you," I said. "Then your dumb planets display might win the science fair!"

"It is *not* dumb!" Polly shrieked. "I've got papier-mâché and everything!"

"All right, people!" Mr. Starchfield called out cheerfully, walking into the classroom. "Let's get learn—" He stopped in his tracks when he saw everyone cowering in front of the blackboard. "What are you all doing standing over there?"

"It's Gus," Polly said, making a face. "He's got his *shoes* off."

I hopped back and forth, rubbing the soles of my feet against my jeans.

"Gus? Whatever are you doing?" Mr. Starchfield demanded. He took a couple of steps toward me, then stopped. As if my feet were going to attack him or something. But the way things were going, I wouldn't have any feet left. The creeping crud was going to eat them alive!

Or dead. They were starting to smell sort of rotten, like a piece of raw meat that falls behind the garbage bin and sits there for days until Mom gets all grossed out and—

Well, anyway. Mr. Starchfield was staring at my bare feet, a look of sheer horror on his face. "Gus? Can you explain?" he asked me, keeping his distance.

"Sure, I can explain," I said. "Yesterday, in gym class, Ray pushed me into the—"

"Pool?" Mr. Starchfield guessed, interrupting me.

"No," I said. "He shoved me into the—"

"Sauna?" Mr. Starchfield said.

"No...Mr. Starchfield, we don't *have* a sauna," I pointed out.

"Oh. No, of course not. I mean, not for students. I mean, not that teachers have one, either!" he added, sounding nervous.

Last year the teachers got into trouble because it turned out they were spending a bunch of our class trip money to fix up their lounge. They bought a cappuccino machine and a brand-new fridge. I wouldn't be surprised if they *did* install a sauna.

"Anyway, Ray didn't push me into the sauna," I said. "He made me land in the—"

"Look, Gus," Ray said. "I didn't do a thing to you. I don't know what you're talking about."

"You're such a liar!" I cried, hopping around the classroom.

"Well, at least I'm not a walking case of toe crud!" Ray shot back.

"Boys! Didn't you learn anything in detention yesterday?" Mr. Starchfield thundered.

"Sure," Ray said. "I learned how to tell time." He guffawed. "And the hour between three and four is longer than any other hour on the clock!"

Polly and a bunch of other kids giggled.

Mr. Starchfield sighed loudly. "Well, Gus, I'm afraid I'm going to have to ask you to go see Nurse Gil—"

"No!" I said. "I already went to see her. I think she made it worse."

"Then how about trying some sort of spray or something?" Mr. Starchfield suggested. "I'm sure Coach K. has a can of—"

I shook my head. "I already tried a spray. In fact, I'm pretty sure I'm having an allergic reaction to it right now!"

"I'll say," Polly said, flipping her hair over her shoulder. "And the rest of us are allergic to *you*." She rubbed her ear for a second. "I'm serious! I'm getting itchy!"

"Gus, I hate to do this. Your education is very important. But at Thornhill, we have a saying," Mr. Starchfield informed me, sounding very serious.

"Bring your lunch or die?" I asked.

A couple of kids laughed—even Ray.

Mr. Starchfield frowned. "No...that's not it. Actually, the one that applies to this situation is as follows: No shirt, no shoes, no school."

He pointed to my bare feet—if you could call them bare, with all that fuzz and ooze coming out from between my toes. "Gus, go home."

"But—" I started to protest.

Mr. Starchfield shook his head. "There are no

exceptions to the rule. If you aren't wearing shoes, you're not allowed to be here. We do have a health code, you know."

Tell that to the lunch ladies! I thought.

I figured old Starchfield was right. If I did go home, maybe I'd find a way to get rid of the junk on my feet. It was driving me crazy. And there was no way I could sit still in class. "Okay, I'll leave," I began.

A loud cheer went up from my classmates.

"But I'm telling you—he stole my science experiment!" I said, pointing at Ray.

Mr. Starchfield dragged me to the door by my collar. He threw my sneakers out into the hall after me. One of them hit me on the rear end!

Boy, Mr. Starchfield can really be a jerk when he wants to be.

When I got home, I filled the bathtub with steaming hot water and stuck my feet in. "Aaaah!"

I stared at the fungus, waiting for it to dissolve in the hot water. Boiling water was supposed to help. Instead, it grew even more!

I dried off my feet with a huge wad of Kleenex, then I ran into Jake's room. Maybe I hadn't put the spray on the right way. Maybe I should have read the directions, I thought. Once I did, I could get rid of this problem and have a *real* day off from school.

I picked up the can from his dresser and read the instructions. WARNING: DO NOT USE IMMEDIATELY AFTER BREAKFAST! There was a bunch of stuff about how the ingredients didn't react with milk. And how it might cause bad side effects.

"Great!" I exclaimed. "Some help this junk is!"

I tossed the can onto the floor and ran back to the bathroom. With all the junk my mom and dad kept in the medicine cabinet, I knew I'd find something.

I stared at all the little bottles on the shelves. FRENCH VANILLA BUBBLE BATH GEL. PEPTIC ULCER PURÉE. BUNION BUZZ-OFF. CANKER SORE KILLER. AGE SPOT REMOVER. LOOK YOUNG GENTLEMAN'S HAIR GROWER.

Boy, did my parents have a lot of problems.

But there wasn't anything in the entire bathroom that would help *me*.

There was only one solution left. I had to go to the drugstore. I ran into my room and spilled the contents of Mr. Piggy on the bed. It came to $9.78.

I was almost out the door when I realized I wasn't wearing any shoes. I needed shoes, or they wouldn't let me in the store. But whenever I put my new sneakers on, it was torture. My fungoid feet needed air to breathe, or the stuff grew even faster!

My dad had some sandals, so I checked out

his closet. The problem was, my dad's feet were about twice as big as mine, and I couldn't walk in his shoes. I looked like a clown.

I found a pair of white open-toe sandals in my mom's closet and slipped them on. I tried walking in them—it was okay. But when I saw myself in the full-length mirror, I looked ridiculous! I was wearing high heels, with a little pink flower on the front of each shoe!

I tossed them back into the closet and went back to my room.

Then I got out a pair of scissors and started cutting off the front ends of my Air Jordans. "Good-bye, cool new sneakers," I said. "Hello, Air Moulders."

"Hello," I said, standing at the pharmacy counter at the back of the drugstore. "I need some help, please."

"Just a minute, young man!" the pharmacist said. "I have one more prescription to fill for Mrs. Mallarque and then I'll be right with you."

I glanced over at the older woman standing beside me. She had nine bottles of stuff on the counter in front of her already. She looked like she was about a hundred and fifty years old. And she must have been taking a pill for everything.

After the pharmacist filled her last prescription, he started going over all the instructions with her. "Now, you take one of these three times a day, two of these once a day, take this with food, and take this on an empty stomach—"

"Just a second, whippersnapper," Mrs. Mallarque said, tapping him on the arm with her cane. "Which one do I take three times a day with food, once a week after lunch but before dinner only on Saturdays?"

I sighed. This was going to take a long time. Maybe I should just look around myself. I headed down the aisle called GENERAL DISCOMFORT.

A couple of girls were coming toward me, carrying bags of chips and cans of sodas. When they got closer, one of them dropped a bag of chips on the floor. "Aaaaaaiiieeee!" she screamed. "Look!"

Her friend shrieked and stepped on the bag of chips. It exploded, and the chips went flying across the floor, crunched to smithereens. "Look what you've done! Get—get out of here!" she yelled.

"What seems to be the problem?" one clerk asked while someone called over the public address system, "Manager to General Discomfort, right away. General Discomfort, near Upset Stomach!"

"He—he—he," the first girl stuttered. She was wheezing and breathing funny. Finally she gave up trying to talk and just pointed to my feet.

"You know," I began, with a nervous glance at the clerk, "it's not *really* as bad as it looks. I just need something to put on them and—"

"Yuck!" The clerk put his hand over his mouth. "That's disgusting. You'd better see a doctor right away."

"But isn't there some type of cure here?" I asked.

The clerk shook his head back and forth so quickly, I thought his brain would fall out.

"Brian?" A tall woman wearing a jacket that had the word MANAGER stitched on it in bright red letters walked up to us. "Is there a problem?"

"Yeah! Like, we're never coming back here!" one of the girls said, and they both ran for the door.

"Hm. Losing customers—over a bag of broken chips?" the manager asked. She leaned over to pick up the bag. That's when she saw them. My feet. Her whole body shuddered, like a car engine trying to start in freezing cold weather.

"You—son—you need to go see a doctor," she said, standing up and looking at me. I could tell she was trying to be cool about it, but her face was turning sort of green.

"Really?" I asked. "Like who?"

She took me by the shoulders and started guiding me to the door.

"I don't know, but you need major help—

46

fast." She passed by the drugstore's bulletin board and pulled down a flier.

"Why don't you try Doctor Dreck?" the manager said, handing me the piece of paper. "He's new around here, but he's supposed to have a cure for everything. He's a dermatologist...maybe he can help you with...whatever it is that you have."

She cleared her throat. "And until that... clears up...we'd appreciate you shopping somewhere else. Like...perhaps by mail. Thank you very much. Good luck. And good-bye," she said in a rush. Then she shoved me out the door and closed it behind me.

I tripped on a rock, stubbing my exposed toe. "Ow!" I cried, reaching down to rub the injured spot. My hand came back covered in puffed white sticky stuff. "Ew!" I said. "Ow! Ew!"

I was starting to sound like a babbling idiot!

I had to find Dr. Dreck right away!

CHAPTER SIX

I was standing in front of the house trying to figure out how to get to Dr. Dreck's office when Jake pulled up in a brand-new, shiny red sports car.

"Where'd you get that?" I asked. "Is it yours?"

"Not yet, but it's going to be," Jake said proudly. "I'm on a test drive. I wanted to see how it handled the driveway."

"Mom and Dad will never buy you that car," I said. "Anyway, our driveway's about two feet long."

"So? It's still important." Jake revved the engine and peeled out, charging up the hill to our garage. When he got to the top, half a second later, he turned to me. "What are you doing home, anyway? Are you sick or something?"

"Not exactly," I said. I pointed to my feet. "Remember that spray you told me to use?"

48

Jake nodded. "What happened to your sneakers?"

"I had to cut them off, after my athlete's foot thing got worse—thanks to you. You didn't tell me the spray's not supposed to be used right after breakfast!" I told him.

"Oh, right." Jake hit himself on the head. "Coach K. did tell me that once. Sorry. I *completely* forgot. Gee, I'm really sorry, Shrimp."

"Yeah, right," I muttered. "I bet you are."

"Well, you know how it is. I have a lot on my mind, what with buying a new car and all." He ran his hand along the sleek car. "I can't be bothered with your little problems."

What did I tell you? He's a jerk. "You know," I began. "I was just standing here thinking about telling Mom and Dad how you almost got me killed by telling me to use that stuff. I mean, I had this horrible allergic reaction. They kicked me out of school, which was totally humiliating, plus I had to ruin my sneakers, which they're not going to like, plus—"

"All right, already. Before you sue me, what do you want?" Jake sighed.

"A ride?" I asked. "I just made an appointment with a doctor, but he's on the other side of town. Drop me off, and I won't say a thing to anyone."

"Get in," Jake said. "But I'll have to drive fast. I have to get the car back."

49

"No problem." I got into the passenger side and was strapping on my seat belt when Jake roared the car into reverse, and we went flying over the curb. "You have your license, right?" I asked, clutching my seat.

"No," Jake said.

"No! What do you mean, no?" I demanded.

"I don't have it," he said.

"Well—why not?"

"I don't have it because I had to give it to the guys at the car lot so they'd let me take the car for a spin," Jake said smugly. He turned to me and winked.

I rolled my eyes and looked out the window until we got to Dr. Dreck's. His office was in the big medical building that was shaped like a giant kidney. Jake dropped me off in front. "You can walk home, right?" he said.

"Well, uh—"

"See ya!" He peeled out of the parking lot, leaving me standing there on the sidewalk. Sure, I could walk home. It would probably take me two hours though!

Shaking my head, I walked into the building. Then I scanned the list of offices posted on the wall by the door.

"'Dr. Herman Dreck,'" I read out loud. "'Dermatology, Diseases of the Skin, and Wart Disposal. Room 113.'"

I headed down the winding hallway until I

reached the end of the kidney. The numbers 113 were written in jagged script on a freshly painted sign and nailed to the door. And there was another sign next to the door that said, MAJOR CREDIT CARDS ACCEPTED, INCLUDING DINER'S CLUB.

That's when I remembered I had only $9.78. I didn't know what Dr. Dreck could do for my foot fungus, but I had to give it a shot. Whatever he charged was going to be too much for me, so I'd just tell him to bill my parents. They'd understand. They'd have to. Or else everyone in the house was going to come down with the fungal nightmare.

I knocked a couple of times on the door and pushed it open. The door hardly moved because there was this thick beige shag rug on the floor. When I finally shoved it all the way open, I almost fell to the floor.

Not because it gave way—but because Polly Petri was sitting in the waiting room!

Polly was perched on a purple plastic chair, looking positively putrid. Polly! The girl who was voted "Most Likely to Become a Supermodel!" Her face was covered with oozing blisters!

"Polly?" I said. "Polly Petri? Is that you?"

CHAPTER SEVEN

"What *happened* to you?" I asked as I walked into the office and took a seat next to her. There was a weird smell in the waiting room—as if something was burning.

Polly put her hands in front of her face. I guess she was feeling self-conscious. But you can't be too concerned about your looks when your face is covered with pus. I mean, it's *going* to show.

"I got poison ivy," she finally said, her voice muffled by her hands.

"You better not touch your face with your hands, then," I said. "It's going to spread!"

"Too late," Polly said, turning her hands over so I could see them. They were covered with red lumps and bumps, half of which had been rubbed raw.

"Wow," I said. "You've got it bad!" I almost found myself admiring Polly. How could she just sit there in that chair, in utter agony? She must be tougher than I'd thought. "How did that happen?"

"I went on a hike after school yesterday, with Ray," Polly said.

"Okay, so my first question is...*why*?" I asked.

"Because he asked me to," Polly said. "And he knew all about this new trail. I thought it would be kind of fun until—"

"Wait—don't tell me!" I said. "He saw a crop of poison ivy and shoved you into it!"

Polly opened her eyes wide. "No. Why would he do that?"

"Oh, uh, no reason," I said. "So what did happen?"

"We were in the park, and we sat down for a while to have a snack—"

"Chips, right?" I interrupted. "Barbecued?"

Polly frowned. "Are you going to let me tell the story or not?"

I guess the poison ivy hadn't infected her snob factor yet. "Sorry," I said. "Go ahead."

"Well, as I was *saying*, we went to the park for a hike, and I brought some cookies. So we sat down to eat them, and I guess I put my hand on a poison ivy plant," she explained. "Then this mosquito flew in my ear, so I went to kill it, and I touched my ear, and that's how it all started."

"But—wait a second," I said. "This was yesterday? How did it spread so fast?"

"I have two words for you," Polly said.

"Bad hygiene?" I guessed.

She sighed. "Hardly. I take showers twice a day. No, I'm talking about Nurse Gillette."

I nodded. "I should have known. She almost burned my feet off with iodine. What did she do to you?" I asked.

"I don't know, but when I went in there, I had poison ivy behind my ear. Now I have it everywhere! She said it's some extra-strength strain or something, that would probably run its course in twenty-four hours. But I can't wait twenty-four hours. Gus, I've been kicked off the cheerleading squad until my face goes back to normal!" She sniffled.

"Wow," I said. Not that I thought it was so amazing, but you should have heard her cry. It was pathetic. I figured she needed a little sympathy. "Well, don't worry, I'm sure Dr. Dreck can make you better," I said.

Tears were rolling down her cheeks, mixing with the pus. She really looked revolting. She blinked a couple of times, then pointed at my feet, which were sticking out the end of my sneakers. "Can't you put socks over those things or something? They're making me sick!"

Sympathy was wasted on someone like Polly. "Well, look in the mirror!" I said. "If I have to look at you for another second, I'm going to barf!"

All of a sudden, a door opened and a nurse with spots on her face marched toward me in a pair of white platform nurse's shoes. She looked as if she had the measles! "Young man, if you're going to sit in my waiting room, I'm going to need your name."

"Gus Moulder," I said, leaning away from her. The last thing I needed was to catch some other disease. I was already taking a risk by sitting next to Polly Poison Ivy. "I have a two o'clock appointment."

She studied the clipboard in her hand, then checked off my name. "Very well then. Please fill out this form and the doctor will be with you shortly." She handed me a sheet of paper with at least fifty questions on it.

"What about me? I have a one-thirty appointment," Polly said. "I should be first, before *him*."

"The doctor's running a bit late. Some stubborn warts, I understand. He's bringing in a blowtorch," the nurse explained.

So that explained the weird burning smell, I thought. Then I panicked. Was he going to fry the fungus off my feet? "Uh, Nurse, you don't know what the treatment would be for, say, athlete's foot, do you?"

"Oh, the doctor uses many methods. I can't begin to imagine what he might do for...your problem." She glanced at my feet, making a face. "Perhaps an iodine treatment would help."

I cleared my throat. "Is your last name Gillette, by any chance?" I asked.

She gave me a puzzled look and shook her head. "No, why?"

"Oh—just wondering. You remind me of someone," I said. Someone else who wears platform shoes and tortures kids!

"Well, here's a pen. Start writing," she instructed me.

I picked up a magazine to put the form on while I wrote. It was the latest issue of *Skin Disease Monthly.* On the cover was a photograph of someone with a pimple the size of Mount St. Helens. Lucky for me, I didn't have acne. Not yet.

I took a pen out of a jar on the table beside me. "Have you ever been convicted of a major crime?" was the first question on the list. "Please answer: Yes, No, Maybe."

I skipped to the next question. "If you were going to rate your skin happiness factor, on a scale of 1 to 10, what would it be?"

I tapped the pen against my chin, thinking. *Zero,* I wrote down. Then I glanced at my feet again and erased what I'd written. *Negative one.*

Suddenly a door opened, and a doctor walked into the waiting room. Dr. Dreck! I thought excitedly. He had a pair of thick, square glasses on his face—the kind that make your eyes look huge. His white coat was starched and pressed precisely, and he had a stethoscope around his neck that was shiny clean.

Then someone came out of the office after him. It was the man with the giant warts! His hair was sticking straight up on his head, and smoke was coming out of the bottom of his pants. And he was shaking all over!

I turned to Polly. Her mouth was wide open, and she watched as the man slowly walked up to the nurse's desk to pay his bill. He definitely looked as if he was in pain!

Dr. Dreck clapped him on the back, and he nearly fell over. "See you next week, James!" he said.

James's leg twitched violently. "Yeah, right. Next week. Sure," he said nervously.

Polly looked at me. "This is the guy who's going to help us?" she whispered.

I chewed my thumbnail and shrugged. "Maybe it's not as bad as it looks?"

Polly's eyebrows shot up. "I thought you were supposed to be smart."

Before I had a chance to defend myself, Dr. Dreck had picked up our charts and was walking toward us. "Kids, I'm a little pressed for time this afternoon. I was wondering if it would be all right if I treated you at the same time, since your conditions are so similar."

"S-similar?" Polly stuttered. "But I have poison ivy. And he has toenail fungus!"

Doctor Dreck put his hand on Polly's shoulder. "Modern medicine can handle both problems. Trust me! Dermatology has come a long way. Come on into my office and we'll get you both set up."

"Dermatology," I muttered to Polly, following her across the waiting room to Dr. Dreck's office. "Did you see that guy with the burned pants? Looks more like derma-torture to me..."

CHAPTER EIGHT

"Just have a seat right here." Dr. Dreck patted two soft-looking tables. "I'll prepare a few treatments for you, and you'll be back to your shiny, sparkling selves in no time. Trust me!"

I looked at Polly, raising one eyebrow. This was the guy who'd just about fried his last patient. And we were supposed to trust him? That's like trusting Ray Roches not to steal your homework.

I wandered around the office, looking at the pictures hanging on the wall. There was one row of photos labeled BEFORE TREATMENT, and another row labeled AFTER! I stared at them, my jaw dropping open. Every single person looked worse *after* treatment than before!

One woman had beautiful, clear skin BEFORE. AFTER seeing Dr. Dreck, she had a wart on her eyelid and a patch of pimples on one cheek!

I was about to run out of there when Polly caught a glimpse of her face in the mirror above the sink. She nearly fainted. I caught her just in time and helped her lie down on one of the tables.

"Yuck!" she cried. "What's this table made out of, anyway?"

"Sea sponges!" Dr. Dreck said. "All natural, and very healthy."

Polly sniffed and said, "Well, it *is* kind of comfortable."

I got onto the other table, and as soon as I lay down on the giant sponge, Dr. Dreck fastened a strap around my waist.

"What's that for?" I asked, biting my fingernails.

"It's simply to keep you in place, so that you don't move around," Dr. Dreck said with a smile.

I chewed my thumbnail. I felt like the monster in *Frankenstein*.

Dr. Dreck strapped Polly onto her sponge, then went to the sink to rinse his hands. He was whistling.

You know that nasty smell sponges get, when you keep them too long? And they're around the sink, and you should probably throw them out and open a new package? Only your mom and dad are too cheap, and they're too old to have much of a sense of smell left?

Well, that's how this sea sponge I was lying on smelled. Gross!

Dr. Dreck walked toward us, carrying a tray. "Now, before I begin, let me tell you what I'm going to do," Dr. Dreck said, setting the tray down at the end of Polly's table. "First, I will apply a mixture of honey, yogurt, granola, and raw eggs to the affected areas. Your face, Gus, and your feet, Polly."

"It's my face—and his feet!" Polly interrupted. "How you could ever confuse us is totally beyond me. I mean, all you have to do is look at his swamp feet—"

"And her blister face!" I added.

"It was a simple error, easily corrected," Dr. Dreck said, stirring the sour-smelling goop in the bowl on his tray. "After a five-minute coating with the honey-egg mixture, you will proceed immediately to the wart wash, followed by a full-body soaking, similar to a flea dip—"

"Flea dip!" Polly exclaimed.

"We don't have fleas!" I protested. "We're not dogs!"

"Nor are you cats," Dr. Dreck said, nodding seriously. At least he had that much figured out! "However, this is a dip I've specially prepared for afflicted skin—sour cream and onion."

"Well, um, isn't that for potato chips?" I asked.

"You're not going to eat it. These preparations will soothe your skin," Dr. Dreck said.

"Okay, fine," I said. "Soothing is good." I rubbed my feet together furiously. The itching was driving me nuts! "But what about curing us?"

"Yeah," Polly said. "That *is* why we're here."

Dr. Dreck lifted the spoon to his lips and tasted the batter. "Mmmmm...yes, I was getting to that. If you'd just be patient—Oh, ha-ha, that was a very good joke, wasn't it? If you'd just be *patient*. But you *are* patients!"

"Ha-ha," I muttered.

"Very funny," Polly mumbled.

Dr. Dreck kept on chuckling. I looked over at Polly. Her face was a combination of peeling skin and oozing pus. My feet didn't look any better.

"So...is that all?" I asked.

"Oh, no. After the honey and eggs, the wart wash, and the flea dip, we'll also have to give you four different vitamin shots, five times a day. Also, you'll have to drink a special kind of juice that I make myself."

Dr. Dreck leaned over to look at Polly's face with a bright flashlight. "Yes, I see lots of juice in your future. A few quarts, definitely." He shined the light on a particularly nasty section of red poison ivy bumps on the end of Polly's nose.

Polly frowned. "What kind of juice?"

"A delicious combination of sea kelp, tomato purée, and witch hazel," Dr. Dreck said. "Then

I'll be giving you both acid peels. In addition to getting rid of all the old, dead skin, the peels will make you look much, much younger—"

"But I'm twelve years old," Polly said. "I don't need to look younger!"

"And I don't care how young my *feet* look!" I said.

"Listen, acid peels are wonderful," Dr. Dreck said, wringing his hands. "Now you two have to relax a little bit. All this stress is only making your conditions worse. I'm going to put on some calming music, and when I come back, I expect you to be ready to begin the process." He glanced at his watch. "My next appointment is in twenty minutes, so we don't have much time. I'll be right back!" He walked out of the room, whistling cheerfully.

"Polly!" I said as soon as the door was closed. "We have to get out of here!"

"No kidding!" she said. "But how? My arms are strapped to this table. I can't get the thing undone!" She was struggling to reach the hook. Every time she squirmed around on the sponge table, brownish-gray water oozed out of it onto the floor with a squishy, sucking sound.

I tried to unhook my strap from the clip on the side of the table. I had almost managed to get it undone when weird music started playing out of these giant speakers on the ceiling.

"What's that?" Polly asked. "It's creepy!"

"It must be his inspirational tape," I said. "The one he listens to before he starts his derma-torture!"

"He said it was supposed to calm us down," Polly complained. "Well, it's time to ask yourself something, Gus. Do you feel *calm*?"

Just then, the door opened and Dr. Dreck strolled back in, rubbing his hands together. "All right then! Let's get this skin on the road! Ha-ha-ha."

He started spooning a whitish-yellowish mixture onto my feet. I gripped the table with both hands, staring at the egg he perched on my big toe.

It broke, and the yolk ran down my foot.

"Oh, gross!" Polly said. "I'm going to puke—"

Before she could say another word, Dr. Dreck covered her face in yogurt, egg yolks, granola, and honey. Tiny clumps of granola clung to her eyelids. She looked like a train wreck!

Polly didn't open her mouth for the next five minutes. Hey, I wouldn't either if I had all that junk on my face.

The yogurt oozed all over my feet, and the granola felt like pebbles between my toes.

"Okay then! Now that your skin's had a chance to absorb the healing goodness of raw eggs, it's time for the wart wash!" Dr. Dreck said excitedly.

"The wart wash?" I asked. "What's that?"

"I don't *have* warts, okay?" Polly protested. "I *know* what my condition is: poison ivy!"

"We can't be too careful," Dr. Dreck said, unstrapping us from the tables. He guided us to a door at the back of his office. "Besides, most of my patients think this is fun! Hop in, kids! Enjoy the ride!"

"Well, I guess it will feel nice to wash this gook off my face," Polly said, wiping an egg yolk off her forehead.

I put one foot into the darkened room—and my toes touched something cold, slimy, and rubbery. I shuddered. It was even more disgusting than the glop on my feet.

Then Dr. Dreck flipped a switch on the wall, and a motor whirred into action, turning on yellow fog lights.

I looked down. I was standing on a moving conveyor belt—heading straight for something that looked like a rubber octopus!

"See you at the other end!" Dr. Dreck yelled over the noise of the machine. Then he closed the door.

Polly tried to run after him, but she slipped on the conveyor belt—and started going through the wart wash on her stomach!

I tried running backward so I could turn off the switch—but the conveyor belt was moving too fast. I couldn't get anywhere.

Polly scrambled to her feet. Just then, these

giant tentacles hanging down from the ceiling started swishing back and forth—and one of them knocked her over! "Aaaah!" she cried. "Gus, help me!" Her hair was about to get stuck in the conveyor belt. The split ends were getting closer and closer to the turning cylinder...

At the last second, I grabbed her arm and pulled her up, holding her hand. She cringed as she saw the rubber strings dangling ahead of us, covered with green slimy soap that looked like the inside of someone's nose. Someone with a really, really bad cold, that is!

That was pretty scary. But what was even more frightening was the fact that I was still holding Polly's hand! "Aaaaah!" I screamed.

I dropped her hand just as the octopus wrapped its arms around us, scrubbing us. Musty-smelling water dripped all over my face from pipes up above. Some kind of stinky disinfectant soap squirted out of a giant porthole on the wall beside Polly—just as she turned to look out of it. The soap squirted right in her face!

"Gus," she gargled. "Hel-l-l-p!"

CHAPTER NINE

"Consider yourselves disinfected!" Dr. Dreck said cheerfully, opening the door at the end of the wart wash.

"Consider yourself sued!" Polly yelled, just before giant, rough brown paper towels shot out of the wall and wrapped around us, rubbing our skin dry—and rubbing off half my skin! Not that it mattered if we were dry, because our *clothes* were totally soaked.

I grimaced as the paper towel went over my face, scrubbing my lip. "Turn this thing off!" I yelled, my voice muffled by the paper towel.

"Gladly." Dr. Dreck smiled at us and flicked a switch high up on the wall that said WART OFF.

"Man!" I exclaimed. "I didn't have warts before, but I probably have them now."

Polly was groping for the wall. "At least you can *see*. Dr. Dreck, I want my money back!"

"Nonsense," Dr. Dreck said with a chuckle. "You haven't even paid me yet. Besides, that soap is chemically designed to dissolve in fifteen seconds."

"What is this, *Mission: Impossible?*" I scoffed.

"Nothing's impossible!" Dr. Dreck declared. "Not when you're a dermatologist. Or was that plastic surgery?...Well, anyway, come right over here, you two. Time to continue your treatment."

"Thanks, but"—I brushed a scrap of black, musty rubber off my shoulder—"I think I've had enough treatment for one day."

"Augustus, it's time to get serious about your health. Do you want the problem cured or not?" Dr. Dreck asked.

"Augustus?" Polly started giggling.

I frowned. I felt like squirting more soap in her eyes, now that she could see again!

"Come on, kids. The worst is over," Dr. Dreck said.

I looked at Polly. She was looking at me. I could tell we were thinking exactly the same thing. We had to get out of there!

"You know, you're right, Dr. Dreck," I said. "The worst *is* over."

"See? Now, that's the kind of positive attitude that'll get you healed!" Dr. Dreck said, slapping me on the back. Then he took his hand away and grimaced, wiping the wart wash slime onto his white coat.

Polly smiled. "The worst is over, and the best is yet to come. That's how I try to look at life."

"Think good thoughts, Doctor Dreck," I said. "Warm, dry thoughts. Warm fuzzies would be good right about now." I grabbed his arm and started pulling him backward through the wart wash, down the slippery sliding belt.

"What are you doing?" Dr. Dreck cried, trying to grab onto the wall. But it was all slimy and he couldn't hold on! "Stop this instant! Nurse!" he yelled.

Polly grabbed a broom from the corner of the office and reached up to turn on the switch to start the wart wash. The motor roared into action, and I jumped off the conveyor belt, leaving Dr. Dreck to go through the giant slippery, musty octopus tentacles.

"But I—I can't swim!" he protested, reaching for us and looking pathetic.

"Who's asking you to swim? Just enjoy the ride!" I said.

"Most of our patients do!" Polly added, turning off the light.

"You won't get away with this!" he cried. "You'll be charged for the whole half hour and—"

"Not if we have our files, we won't!" I said. I grabbed our folders, threw open the door, and ran into the waiting room.

The nurse sitting at the desk looked up at me

and Polly. "All better? Will that be cash or charge?" she asked.

"We'll send you a check!" Polly said, and we charged into the hallway. We wound our way around the giant kidney-shaped building until we reached the spleen. Then we ran out the exit.

We didn't stop running until we got to the end of the block. "I hope he drowns in there!" Polly panted, trying to catch her breath.

I nodded, wiping a trickle of sweat off my forehead. "I hope he gets foot fungus *and* poison ivy!"

We were standing on the corner when Jake pulled up, this time in a tiny blue convertible. "Gus! What happened at the doc's?"

"We almost got killed, that's what happened," I said.

"There's always some story with you, isn't there?" Jake asked.

"What are you doing here?"

"I felt bad about stranding you," Jake said. "Plus, I decided to take the afternoon off from school to do some more test drives." He looked at Polly for a second, as if he'd just noticed her. "Well, well. You didn't have a doctor's appointment after all, did you? You came over here to meet your girlfriend, didn't you?"

"Who are you, Sherlock Holmes?" I shook my head. "This is Polly. She's not my girlfriend. She's just...someone from school, that's all."

"Oh, right." Jake looked at me and winked. "I'm sure." He gestured for me to walk toward the car, so I did. When I got closer, he whispered, "Normally I'd congratulate you, Gus, seeing as how it's your first date and all. But that girl is weird-looking. What happened to her face?"

"It's just poison ivy," I said. "It'll clear up. She's very pretty, actually."

"Ooh, sensitive, are we?" Jake teased me.

"Just get lost!" I said.

"Okay, fine. *Don't* have a ride home," Jake said. Then he peeled out, speeding away down the street.

"Nice going," Polly said with a sigh. "Now what are we going to do?"

I shrugged. "Walk?"

"But we'll have to walk for miles, and part of it is on the four-lane highway, where there's no sidewalk," Polly groaned.

"Believe me, it's safer than driving with my brother," I said. I couldn't believe he'd taken off! What a jerk!

"Gus, you realize this isn't the end, don't you?" Polly asked me when we reached her house. She looked really upset. "I mean, it's not over between us. It can't be!"

What? I thought. Did Polly want to go out with me? "You mean you and me? You don't want *us* to...end?" I asked.

71

"Don't kid yourself. No, not us. There *is* no us. What I meant was our poison ivy and fungus situation!" Polly said, sounding frustrated. "We've got to try something else. If I don't get back to normal soon, I can forget about going to high school. I'm going to have so many craters and scars on my face, you could play Connect the Dots."

I smiled, picturing Polly with a bunch of ink lines drawn on her face. "Yeah, well, at least you can wear shoes," I said.

Polly rolled her eyes. "At least you can cover up your problem."

"Yeah, but when I do, it gets worse," I said.

"There has to be something we can do," Polly said. "I know! We can use my dad's computer to surf the Web and see if there's any information on curing us."

"You mean…like the Poison Ivy Home Page?" I asked. "Or the Toenail Fungus Network?"

Polly put her hands on her hips. "Look, it's a good idea. And I can do this all myself. You can go find your own cure under a bush or something on the way home, for all I care."

I sighed. "No, I'll come with you." What a pus face.

I followed her down the hall to her father's office. On the way, we passed by a small room that had a bunch of different-colored balls on a table. They were all different sizes, and they looked homemade. One even had rings around it.

I stopped in the hallway, peeking in. "Is that your planet project for the science fair?" I asked. "Wow, you've even got Saturn."

"Don't look in there," Polly said and closed the door.

"Why not? It's not like I'm going to steal your idea," I said with a laugh.

"I just don't want anyone to see it before the fair," Polly said.

"Well, at least you're almost done. I don't even have anything for the science fair, now that Ray stole my prize mold," I told her. "I have to come up with something right away."

"That's why you shouldn't look at my project," Polly declared. "Follow me."

Boy, if I didn't know better, I would have thought Polly was a lot like me. I didn't like anyone looking at my projects, either. Maybe she was smarter than I'd thought. She hadn't entered the science fair the past couple of years—maybe she was planning a big comeback!

But I didn't have time to get nervous about that. Anyway, it was simply a matter of me getting rid of my foot fungus and then choosing a replacement mold. The only problem was, when Mother Nature made *Moldus Maximus,* she really did break the mold.

I sat down next to Polly at the computer. She turned it on and started punching in all these codes. She really knew what she was doing! I sat back and watched as she cruised through different Web sites, looking for information. Finally she landed at the "Home Health Help" site. DOCTORS ARE USELESS AND UNNECESSARY! it said in big letters at the top. TRY OUR TIME-TESTED CURES!

"This looks good," Polly said, skimming the "Help" list. "Here we go—Skin."

While Polly was tapping the keys, I started biting my fingernails again—and realized they'd been taken over by fungus! No wonder they'd been bugging me so much! They were covered with green junk and white puffballs.

"Polly!" I cried. "Look!" I held out my hands.

She turned around and her eyes widened in horror. "Gus! Put some gloves on or something!"

"I can't help it," I said.

"Well, you'd better leave before you get any of that crud on me," Polly said angrily.

"Just hurry up and find out the cure, and I'll be glad to," I said. "I don't want to catch your creepy poison ivy, either."

She turned back around and looked up some more information. "'Keep the area as clean and dry as possible,'" she read out loud. "That's all it says! 'Affected area will clear in 48...72 hours.'"

"Four thousand eight hundred seventy-two

hours?" I said. "Polly, we'll be"—I did a quick calculation in my head—"half a year older by then!"

"No, stupid. Forty-eight hours to seventy-two hours," Polly said. "That's two to three days."

I folded my arms across my chest. "That's *not* what you said."

"Well, it's what I meant," Polly said, irritated. "Keep the area dry. Will that work? Let's see what else is on here." She tapped some more keys and brought up more and more screens, flying through them at warp speed. Did this girl know computers or what?

"Gus, they all say the same thing," Polly whined. "Keep the area dry and clean!"

"So?" I shrugged. "What's wrong with that?"

"If we have to keep it dry...that means we can't take showers, or wash our hair—or anything!" Polly wailed.

"Sure we can. We'll just...put plastic on or something," I said. "Like when you have a cast and—"

"Gus, I don't have a broken arm, I have a broken face!" Polly interrupted. "And if I put plastic on it, I won't be able to breathe!"

"Oh, yeah." I thought about it for a second. If I put plastic on my feet and took a shower, they'd probably just get all steamy, like a sauna. And that would make the fungus grow even more! Now that it was on my hands, too, I'd have to put plastic on my hands. I wouldn't be able to hold on to the soap. I'd probably slip, fall down, and drown! So I couldn't bathe, either.

Cool! I liked this cure.

"No way," Polly said. "I'm not going to do this. There has to be some other way to get rid of it!" She stood up and started pacing around the study.

"Look, Polly. You read the same stuff I did. You know what we have to do," I said, sliding my chair back and getting to my feet.

She shook her head. "N-no. Gus, don't make me. I can't. It's too much of a sacrifice."

"Polly! Think of what you're saying!" I stared her right in the eye, like the tough sergeants in the movies did when their troops weren't paying attention.

"I can't do it!" she wailed.

"Do you want to go through life with a pus face?" I demanded. "Do you want to wear a scarf from here to eternity? Do you want the United States of America to be humiliated in front of the entire free world? Well, do you, soldier? Huh?"

Polly took a step away from me, looking concerned. "Gus, I think that fungazoid is spreading to your *brain*."

I cleared my throat. "Polly, come on. You either stop taking showers twice a day...or you end up getting voted 'Most Likely to Model as a Pie Crust!' Which is it going to be?"

Polly tapped her fingernails against the desk. "I don't know..."

"Think about the squad! The other cheerleaders need you!" I said. "The pyramid is totally ruined without you!"

She looked at me, her eyes brimming with tears. "Okay. I'll do it," she finally said. "But don't expect me to like it."

I pointed to the box of tissues on her father's desk. "Don't take any showers, and *don't* cry," I said. "Otherwise, it'll never work."

"Okay, okay. Just *don't* sit next to me in class," Polly said, making a face.

"You don't even have to ask," I said. I wondered which one of us was going to smell worse!

This could turn out to be my best experiment ever!

CHAPTER TEN

"Breakfast!" my mother yelled.

I threw off the covers and looked at my feet. Almost all the fungus was gone! "Mom!" I cried. "Mom, it's gone!"

"And so am I!" she said. "Your breakfast will be in the garage, as usual. Right near your...fungi collection."

I heard her running off down the hall. She hadn't seen me in person for three days. I was being quarantined in my own home. I kind of missed my family, but the cure was working!

I was really getting into this not bathing routine. How long could a human body go, anyway, without being washed? Maybe this could be my new experiment for the science fair!

Jake pounded on the door. "Shrimp! Hey, Shrimp!"

"Yeah?" I called back.

"I want to ask you something," he said through the crack in the door.

I got out of bed and started getting ready for school. Now that I wasn't taking showers, it was much faster. "So, go ahead," I said, pulling on my clothes.

"How's your ugly girlfriend?" Jake started laughing. "Is she in prison at her house, too?"

"She's not my girlfriend," I said. "Why don't you go do something useful? Like maybe donate your passing arm to science?"

"Oh, ha-ha," Jake said. "I see that fungal thing has started spreading to your brain!"

"At least I have one!" I said.

"Well, you—you—" Jake stammered. "You... you're green!"

"Maybe I am today, but tomorrow *I'll* be normal. And *you'll* still be stupid!" I yelled.

"Huh?" Jake said, sounding confused.

I opened the door and pushed my still-crusty fingernails in his face. "Out of my way!"

He flattened himself against the wall so that he was as thin as a Pop-Tart.

I hurried downstairs, wearing the special paper slippers my mother was making me wear around the house. Then I walked out to the garage, going right over to greet my mold collection. "Good morning, macaroni and cheese from—hey, wait a second. What happened to you?"

I stopped, halfway to my *Russula fragrantissima*. There was something wrong! My molds were all covered with some kind of dark soot—and they hadn't grown at all!

Just then the big garage door opened, and Jake walked in to get his car for school. He hadn't gotten the cute little red sports car or the sharp blue convertible he wanted, after all. Jake was now the proud owner of a large four-door car that looked as if it ought to be driven by my grandmother. It was powder blue, with a white top, and got about two miles for every gallon of gas.

"Stay away from me," Jake muttered.

"Where are you taking the boat today?" I asked as he opened the car door.

"Shut up, Shrimp," Jake said. "At least I don't have to walk. At least *I* don't belong in a circus." He turned on the motor, revving the engine. Black smoke shot out the tailpipe—right onto my fungus collection! It was Jake! He was killing them all!

"Murderer!" I cried, shaking my fist.

Jake pulled out of the garage, flooring it. Another spurt of soot landed on my foot as I ran after him. "Come back here! Jake! You killed my molds!"

One of our neighbors, Mr. Knowles, was just picking up his morning newspaper from his front porch. "Gus?" he said. "You all right, son?"

"Oh, hi, Mr. Knowles," I said. "I'm okay. But

Jake just ruined all my future science experiments," I complained. "With his dumb new car!"

"That is quite a clunker," Mr. Knowles said. "I bet it won't last very long. Anyway, you're so smart, I'm sure you'll come up with some more experiments. Well, I gotta go!" He waved and then disappeared behind his front door.

I waved back. Maybe Mr. Knowles was right—maybe Jake's car wouldn't survive. And if it happened to have a flat tire one day...or have some wires cut in half...I'd just say that it was revenge.

Revenge of the Molds!

"I don't want her on my team! She smells!"

"Well, I sure don't want him on my team! He stinks!"

Those were the first words Polly and I heard when we broke for recess that morning. We stood beside the soccer field together while everyone else played.

Polly had a flowered scarf tied around her head to cover her greasy hair and face. But the grease was kind of seeping through anyway—the scarf looked like the bottom of a pizza box.

"So, how's it going?" I asked her.

"Pretty good," she said, scratching her head briefly. "My face is almost all peeled off!"

I shook my head. "That sounds weird. I mean, is that good news?"

"Yeah. It's all the infected junk coming off. See?" She pushed the scarf back a little and turned toward me. Then she peeled a giant strip of skin from under her eye, all the way down to her mouth. "Good-bye, poison ivy!" she said, tossing the dead skin onto the ground.

I noticed that there was a pile of skin where we were standing. It was like hanging out with a shedding snake.

"How're your feet?" she asked.

"They're great," I said, wiggling my toes in my cut-off sneakers. "The green stuff is turning yellow, which means it's almost healed."

"They look like rotten bananas," Polly said, making a face.

"And you're peeling like one!" I laughed.

"Only one more day," she said, crossing her fingers. "And we're home free."

"Fungus free, you mean," I said.

"Whatever! I just want people to stop leaving cans of deodorant on my desk!" Polly said.

"Well, if it isn't the walking, talking, stinking fungus," Ray said to me as we walked back into class after recess.

"Not to mention his disgusting peeling twin," Janie Jones chimed in.

"You two are really revolting, you know that?" Ray said.

82

"You forgot nauseating," Janie said, pinching her nose closed. "You smell like the zoo!"

"It's medical, okay?" I said, sliding into my seat in front of Ray.

"Since when is stinking like an old piece of cabbage medical?" Janie demanded.

Polly adjusted the scarf on her head, moving the greasy spot from one side to the other. "It's only for one more day. And we can't do anything about it—"

"Try a bar of *soap!*" Janie said, her voice all nasal. "Like, as soon as possible!"

"Yeah, maybe you should go to the locker room," Ray suggested. "And take a shower. I mean, it's so nice and clean in there. I can get you a towel after I finish wiping off the floor!" He started laughing.

"You'll pay for this," I muttered through clenched teeth.

"Excuse me, but I think we're paying already!" Janie said. "Like, the air that we breathe is being totally polluted by you two weirdos!"

"Well, at least we aren't adding to the *noise* pollution around here, by yelling and saying rude things!" Polly retorted.

"Rude! You're telling me *I'm* rude?" Janie's face turned bright red. "Do you know what Miss Manners says about washing behind your ears?"

"I don't know, but I know what she says about girls with red hair and freckles who think they're all that—"

"Whoa, whoa! Girls!" I said, holding up my hands. "Let's not fight." I went over to Polly's desk. "Maybe we should just leave. You know, pretend we're sick. Only we are sick, so it wouldn't be pretending."

Polly's face lit up. A couple of skin flakes fell to the floor when she smiled. "That sounds like a good idea. But I don't know." She reached up and scratched her head.

Maybe it was the power of suggestion—you know, seeing her scratch her head? But all of a sudden I had this urge to scratch my head, too. It was itching—out of control! Even more than the fungus had! I scratched my scalp again.

Polly was scrubbing her head, too—nonstop.

"I guess this is what happens when you stop taking showers," I said.

"Yeah. Itchy, greasy scalp," Polly said, scratching her forehead. "It happens on commercials all the time."

I rubbed the side of my head. "So all we need is some shampoo?"

"Yeah. Rinse and repeat!" Polly said. She looked up at me. "Gus?"

"Yeah?" I said.

"I feel like I have mosquitoes on my head," she said. "I know it's crazy, but would you mind looking, just to make sure?"

"Polly, you're imagining things," I said. "You're just not used to being dirty. This horrible itching feeling is totally normal."

"Still…would you mind checking?" she asked.

I sighed, scratching behind my ear. "Well, okay. But hurry up—Starchfield's coming."

Polly untied the scarf and slipped it down around her neck. I reeled backward. Her hair looked like lo mein noodles, but even greasier.

"Well? What do you see?" she asked.

"Hold on a second," I said.

"Yo, Polly! The shine from your head is blinding me!" Ray shouted. "Put your scarf back on!"

"Shut up!" Polly said. "It's your fault I got poison ivy in the first place!"

"My fault?" Ray asked. "Since when is everything bad that happens in this classroom *my* fault?"

"Since September!" everyone yelled at once.

I used the distraction to inspect Polly's head. I felt like Dr. Derma-torture Dreck as I leaned over, peering at her scalp. Fortunately, there was a giant fluorescent light right above her desk, so it was easy to see what was going on in there.

A party! A party of five! Five lice were squirming around, dancing on her head! I rubbed my eyes, looking again. Could it really be that Polly Petri had lice?

I scratched my head, trying to figure out how

to break the news to her. Polly was definitely gong to lose it when she found out.

All of a sudden, I felt something in my hair. I felt around my head and then looked at my hand. There was a live creature—a louse! I stared at it, amazed. I'd never seen one up close before. And it would almost be interesting—if it hadn't infested my head!

"Gus! What are you waiting for? Is there something up there or not?" Polly demanded. She scratched her head, and a tiny louse fell onto her desk. "Aaaah!" she screamed. "What is *that*?"

"It's…it's a louse, I think," I said, leaning over to whisper in her ear. "I think we've got lice."

"No!" she shrieked, and she sank onto the floor in a heap.

"Gus, I *told* you not to ask her to the movies," Ray joked. "I told you she'd say no!"

I tapped her on the cheek. "Come on, Polly. Come on, wake up."

Her eyes popped open. "I'm awake, okay? I just don't want to be!" She groaned. "Tell me this is all a dream!"

"All what's a dream?" Mr. Starchfield walked into the room, swinging his briefcase onto the desk. "Good morning, people! Let's get learning!" He stared at Polly, who was still lying on the floor—and at me, crouching over her. "Would you two please take your seats? Remember—the first to learn is the fastest to earn!"

I pulled Polly to her feet. "We—we can't stay, actually," I said. "We have to go."

Janie Jones stood up and started clapping. "Yes! They have to go!"

"Well, er, you need my permission," Mr. Starchfield said. "Tell me—where are you going? What seems to be the problem? If it's not serious, I'll have to ask you to stay—"

"No!" Janie wailed. "No, they can't stay!"

"We need oxygen in here!" Ray added.

I walked up to Mr. Starchfield and whispered in his ear. "Head lice. Ever heard of it?"

"I'd be happy to issue you hall passes!" Mr. Starchfield said. He quickly scribbled the notes, writing "For as long as they want!" on both. "Good luck!"

"Hey, no fair—why do they get to leave?" Ray complained.

"Trust me, Ray. You don't want to be in their shoes," Mr. Starchfield said. He glanced down at my cut-off sneakers. "Especially not his. Now, out of here, both of you!" He clapped his hands together, dismissing us.

"And don't come back!" Janie yelled.

"You know what this means, don't you?" I said once we were outside in the hall.

Polly turned toward me, trying not to scratch her head. "We aren't going to win Most Attractive Couple in the yearbook?"

"No," I said. "It means we have two choices.

87

Either we go back to Dr. Dreck—"

"Derma-torture?" Polly scratched vigorously behind her ear. "No way, Gus. Never! "

"Okay then. That only leaves us one choice. Nurse—"

"No!" Polly screamed. "Not Nurse Gillette!"

CHAPTER ELEVEN

"I never thought I'd come back here." I took a deep breath. "Ready?"

Polly shrugged. "Ready as I'll ever be. Considering." She frowned at the plaque on the door.

NURSE GILLETTE, it said in big letters. NEVER SAY NEVER!

I rapped on the door a few times with my knuckles. With any luck, Nurse Gillette would be out sick, and there would be a nice, friendly nurse in her place.

The door swung open. No such luck. Nurse Gillette stared down at us from her platform shoes, with her hands on her hips. "You two!" she exclaimed. "Again?"

"Yes, again," Polly said.

"Well, you're only allowed one visit per school term," Nurse Gillette said. "Sorry!" She started to close the door, but I stuck my foot in the way before she could close it.

Not that it stopped her—she tried to shove it closed anyway!

"Hey!" I cried. "That hurts!" She was jamming the door right against my bare toes. I could feel the nails digging into my skin!

She opened the door, and I nearly fell over from the throbbing pain. "Stubborn, are you? Do you want me to show you the school rules?" She stared at Polly.

"Do you want the whole school to get head lice?" Polly retorted.

Nurse Gillette's right eyebrow started twitching. "Head—head lice?" she repeated. "Is that what you said?"

I nodded. "We've both got it. And if you don't help us—"

She grabbed us both by the back of our shirts and dragged us into her office. Then she bolted the door closed behind her and leaned against it! "Did you say what I think you said?"

"Yes, we have lice," I said.

She cringed. "Oh, no. Not again," she muttered. "Never again. I promised myself."

"What do you mean, *again*?" Polly asked. "We didn't have this before. I had poison ivy, remember? Which you gave me the wrong cure for."

"And I had toenail fungus and athlete's foot,"

I reminded her. "And you made me take a bath in iodine."

Nurse Gillette staggered toward the examination table. I don't think she'd heard a word we said. She climbed up on the table and laid her head on the tiny pillow, with her big feet dangling off the end. "It happened five years ago," she began.

"What happened?" I asked.

"Does she think she's talking to a shrink or something?" Polly asked me.

"I didn't mean for it all to go so wrong!" she wailed.

"Nurse Gillette?" I said. "Are you okay?"

"There was a lice outbreak at the last school where I worked," she said.

I let out a deep breath. Was that all?

"Big surprise," Polly said under her breath.

"It started in the second grade. I don't know how!" Nurse Gillette said. "I mean, I wasn't there. I swear I wasn't!" She gulped back a sob.

She sounded like a walrus trying to talk. Her face was all red and wet from crying, and her nurse's cap was crushed against the pillow.

"I didn't think it was serious. I gave them some medicine. I treated them as best as I could!" she sobbed. "But somehow it didn't work. They stayed in their class, and the entire second grade got lice. And then the third...and the fourth..."

"And let me guess. The fifth?" Polly asked.

Nurse Gillette nodded, sniffling. "The fifth grade, too."

"So what happened?" I asked. "Did the whole school get a week off or something?"

"They had to close the school for a month," she said. "And when they reopened...they told me not to bother coming back. The whole town would stop and point at me. They'd cross to the other side of the street when I was near them...there was even an article about me in the local paper...I had to leave town."

"Wow. Cool," I said.

Nurse Gillette abruptly sat up. "It was *not* cool! It was the most horrible time of my life!" She waved her fist in the air. "I had to summon every ounce of my personal strength and integrity just to get up every morning and face a new day!"

"Oh," I said. "Well, whatever. It's over, right?" I smiled uneasily.

She adjusted her smashed cap and brushed the tears off her face. "Yes, it is over. And there's no sense swelling on the past—I mean, dwelling." She shook her head. "It's just that when I heard you two make that joke about lice, it sent me back—"

"It's no joke," Polly said. "Take a look." She bent her head underneath Nurse Gillette's desk lamp.

"N-not a joke?" Nurse Gillette asked, looking hopefully at me.

I shook my head. It was bugging me quite a bit. Or should I say *they* were bugging me—the bugs, I mean. "Nope. We're dead serious."

"Look!" Polly urged.

I couldn't believe she was actually begging Nurse Gillette to help her. Usually we're begging to get out of there!

Nurse Gillette pulled on a pair of plastic gloves from the box on the wall. Then she pushed Polly facedown on the desk.

"Hey!" Polly cried, her voice muffled by the desk blotter. "I'm on a stapler!"

"Sorry." Nurse Gillette pulled her up by the hair, cleared a spot on the desk, then pushed her face back down. "Is that better?"

"Ow," Polly moaned.

"Just hurry up and check out the lice, okay?" I urged.

Nurse Gillette scraped Polly's scalp with the glove. Then she held her finger up in front of the light. "Hm," she said. "It could be..." she said. Then she put whatever she had onto a slide and slipped it under her microscope.

"Can I stand up now?" Polly asked.

Nurse Gillette didn't answer. Her eye was pressed up against the microscope viewer. She wasn't budging. I didn't even think she was breathing.

"Hey! Did you fall asleep or what?" I asked.

"Maybe she's dead!" Polly cried.

Slowly, Nurse Gillette pushed the microscope away from her. "No, I'm not dead," she said in this very quiet, creepy voice. "But those little eggs are going to be!"

"Eggs?" I asked. "I thought we had lice."

"You've got your present-day lice, and your future lice," Nurse Gillette said, opening her top desk drawer.

"Future lice?" Polly asked.

It sounded like a horror movie. *Future Lice, Future Lice 2,* and *Back to the Future Lice.*

"Does that mean these egg things are going to, like, *hatch?* In my *hair?*" Polly asked in horror.

Nurse Gillette shook her head. "Not if I have anything to say about it."

"Which you do, right? Because you're the school nurse and if you don't do something to stop this, it's going to spread all over again, and you might be out of a job, and then you'd have to leave town, and it would be too late for us, and I'd never be able to show my face, never mind my hair, and my career would be over—"

"Polly! Take a breath!" I yelled, shaking her shoulders.

Her face looked really pale, and she started sinking to the floor. She has a habit of doing that. I think maybe she's missing part of her spine or something.

"Gus, Polly, have a seat," Nurse Gillette instructed us. "I know what to do, and I've got to do it right now."

I cleared my throat. "This wouldn't involve iodine, would it?"

"No, no, nothing like that," Nurse Gillette said. "You two sit down, and I'll be right over."

I sank into a chair, eying the bolted door. Even if I wanted to get out, I couldn't. Besides, where would I go? To a school where lice and fungus infections were accepted?

Polly took a seat next to me. "I don't know what she's going to do, but it better work."

Suddenly Nurse Gillette pulled something out of her desk. "Aha! Here it is!" She flicked a switch, and a motor started revving. "It's a good thing this is all charged up. I'll need all the energy it has!"

"What is that?" Polly asked. "A lice killer?"

"In a word?" Nurse Gillette said, walking over to us. "No. It's not. It's a razor. An electric one. Well, technically, it's cordless."

"Wait a second," I said. "What are you planning to do with that?"

"I'm going to shave your heads, what else?" Nurse Gillette said. She put one hand on Polly's head. "Now, hold steady. This won't hurt a bit..."

95

CHAPTER TWELVE

"Noooooo!" I yelled, holding my head. I was too young to be bald.

"What am I thinking?" Nurse Gillette put the razor down on her desk, switching it off.

I heaved a giant sigh of relief. "I knew you weren't that bad," I said nervously. "I always told everyone—Nurse Gillette's really an okay person, just give her a chance—"

"I have to prepare your scalps first," Nurse Gillette said, rooting around in the wall cabinets. "Otherwise you'll get razor burn!"

"Razor burn is the least of our problems," I muttered.

"What are you talking about? You're a guy. Guys can be bald. But not girls!" Polly said.

Nurse Gillette knocked a few bottles over, and they crashed to the floor. Horrible smells came out of them, and I tried not to breathe.

"Now, where did I put that?" she mumbled, searching through the cabinets.

"Look—we've got to get out of here!" Polly said to me. "Or else we're going to look like Mr. and Ms. Clean!"

"Yes, that's right, Polly—you'll be very, very clean when I'm through with the head-shaving," Nurse Gillette said. "It's the first step in the cure."

"But...not everyone with lice gets all their hair cut off," I said, remembering a kid I'd known in third grade. "You can just give them medicine, can't you? And then wash all their stuff like their clothes and sheets and—"

"No!" Nurse Gillette shrieked, turning toward us, her eyebrow twitch starting back up with renewed force. "That's what I tried last time. And look what happened! No, I was a fool for believing! I won't make the same mistake twice!"

"Okay..." I said slowly. Get a grip, Gillette! I thought.

"I can't find any shaving cream. But I'm sure I can come up with a substitute," she said, opening a small refrigerator.

"How about a substitute *nurse*?" Polly complained.

"We'd even take a nurse in training," I said. "Or a candy striper. Is there a candy striper in the house?" I called.

"Really, Gus. I think those lice have gone

straight to your head," Nurse Gillette said, taking out a large white plastic container.

That's the problem! I thought, eyeing her carefully. "What's in that, and what are you going to do with it?" I asked.

"That's for me to know and you to find out," Nurse Gillette said proudly. "Trust me!"

Polly and I stared at each other, eyes open wide.

Trust Nurse Gillette? In what universe? We might have lice-head, but we weren't crazy!

"I'll be using this pain yogurt—I mean, plain yogurt—to prepare your scalps for the shaving," Nurse Gillette said, taking a large metal spoon out of her desk drawer.

"I—uh—I'm allergic to yogurt," Polly said. "You know, that thing where you can't eat milk and dairy products?"

"Lactose intolerant?" Nurse Gillette asked, her brow furrowed.

Polly nodded eagerly. "Yeah! That! And if you can't prep my scalp, you really shouldn't shave it, right?"

"You won't be eating the yogurt," Nurse Gillette explained. "You'll be wearing it. The live cultures will not reach your stomach."

"Live cultures?" I said. "I don't know, those smell pretty dead to me." I didn't know it was possible for yogurt to curdle, but this stuff had definitely passed into another world. It had *already* reached my stomach—I felt like I was going to puke!

"Nonsense, Gus. This is one of nature's healthiest sour foods. Now, Polly, I'm just going to put a healthy dollop right here..." She scooped up a big spoonful of yogurt and started walking toward Polly's head.

"You can't put that on her head!" I said. "It's gone bad."

"Augustus, we're not having lunch. We're saving Thornhill Middle School from a lice outbreak!" Nurse Gillette said. "Now let me do my work!"

I glanced at Polly, who was watching the spoon travel toward her with dread. Her eyes were crossed as she watched the yogurt come closer and closer to her head.

I pictured her without any hair.

Then I pictured me, without any hair, sitting in front of Ray. I'd probably end up with a face drawn on the back of my head. Not to mention orange chips stuck to it. He'd call me Bowling Ball, or Grandpa Goose.

I couldn't let that happen.

"You know what, Nurse Gillette?" I stood up, startling her. "Our hall passes just expired. Excuse us!" I grabbed Polly's arm and pulled her out of the chair.

She knocked Nurse Gillette's hand so that the extra-sour yogurt went right onto her face. "You kids get back here right now!"

I threw open the bolted lock on the door. "Or what?" I asked.

She picked up the razor. "Or it's good-bye, eyebrows!" She paused a minute. "Wait a second. Do lice spread to eyebrows?"

"Come on, Polly—let's go!" I yelled.

We took off down the hall, running as fast as we could.

CHAPTER THIRTEEN

"Stop! In the name of science, stop!" Nurse Gillette screeched. Her white nurse shoes were squeaking like giant mice as she plowed down the hall after us.

I don't know how she can even walk in those platforms, much less run. They had to be size 13, at least. I figured her military training helped—she was probably used to running in boots.

The revving motor of the cordless razor was getting louder and louder. She was carrying it as if she was a runner in the Olympics, and it was the torch. As if she could even qualify!

"What should we do?" I asked Polly.

"Run!" Polly replied.

"I know that, but where?" I said, jogging beside her.

"As far as we can get from *her!*" Polly looked

over her shoulder. "Gus, she's got the razor and the yogurt! She's serious!"

"Of course she's serious," I said. "She doesn't want to get fired again!"

"She doesn't care about us—she only cares about her job!" Polly said.

"And this is *news* to you?" I asked.

"Stop! I said, stop, before—before—before a dangerous situation occurs!" Nurse Gillette yelled.

We were just passing by the teachers' lounge. It was lunchtime. Mr. Starchfield must have heard her, because he came running out of the lounge, looking concerned. "What is it? What happened?" He stared at us, then turned to Nurse Gillette. "What did they do?"

"They refused treatment!" she told him. "And it's a matter of life and death. I've got to get this yogurt on their heads, stat!"

"Maybe I can help!" Mr. Starchfield said, and started running beside her.

I turned around to look at them. Mr. Starchfield was lifting his knees up to his chest with each step. He looked like a weird ostrich.

"What seems to be the problem?" Principal Dane had just come out of her office, followed by her secretary, Lucille. "Nurse?"

"The suspects have refused lawful treatment!" Nurse Gillette said. "And they're being selfish and putting everyone else in danger!"

"Yeah, well, at least I'm not wearing platform shoes!" Polly called over her shoulder. "They went out of style like centuries ago!"

"You can insult my profession, but you can't insult me!" Nurse Gillette yelled back.

"I think she got it backward," I said to Polly. "So much for being the noble nurse."

"The only oath she ever took was to be as mean as possible," Polly agreed.

We turned a corner and started racing down another hall. I was starting to get kind of tired. I didn't know how much longer I could outrun Nurse Gillette, Mr. Starchfield, Principal Dane, and Lucille. Then the janitor came around the corner, almost knocking us down with his broom!

"Kids! What are you doing? No running in the halls!" he said. Then he started chasing us, too!

"I know!" Polly cried. "Let's go into the cafeteria!"

"Huh?" I said. "I thought we were trying *not* to get killed."

"We'll be safe!" Polly said. "The adults never go in there, remember?"

I nodded. She was right! I hadn't seen Mr. Starchfield or Principal Dane in the cafeteria since the Sloppy Joe incident, when Ray had put Sloppy Joes, sloppy side up, on all the teachers' chairs right before they sat down. "Okay! Let's do it!" I said.

We rounded the corner and ducked into the

first cafeteria door. I pinched my nose closed as soon as we ran in, so that I couldn't smell the fumes from the putrid food. I had enough problems without worrying about spewing, too.

"Back here?" Polly said, heading for the lunch line.

"Back there!" I cried, looking around at everyone sitting in the cafeteria. Half of the kids were so pale and unhealthy-looking, they were practically invisible. "But—"

"This is no time for a weak stomach," Polly commanded. "Come on!"

I crouched behind a large tray of mushy canned string beans. They smelled so salty, it was like being near the ocean. Beside the beans was a tray of mashed potatoes. At least I think it was potatoes. There was this gray jelly on top—I think it was supposed to be gravy.

"Gus!" Polly gasped.

"What? Are they coming?" I asked, peering over the green beans.

She shook her head. "No—look!"

She pointed at a lump in the next tray over. It was the giant meat loaf—the same meat loaf they'd served for our "Welcome Back to School!" meal at the end of summer vacation. Which was weeks ago! And they were still serving it!

Talk about leftovers! More like "left for dead!"

"No wonder our class has been getting smaller," I said to Polly.

"Shhh." She put her finger to her lips and gestured to the doorway. I peeked over the top of the tray. The door burst open and Nurse Gillette rushed in first, still holding the yogurt and the razor.

"Ooh! Can I have some of that?" a girl asked, taking the yogurt container from her.

I couldn't blame her. It was probably fresher than anything else in the room!

Mr. Starchfield jogged into the cafeteria next. He looked around frantically. "Gus? Polly? Come on, people. When you run away from problems, you run away from solutions!"

I looked at Polly and rolled my eyes. But she was too busy scratching her head to notice.

The janitor ran into the cafeteria, brandishing his broom. Behind him was Principal Dane. Lucille burst into the cafeteria last. She took one look around and passed out, sinking to the floor in a heap of pink chiffon.

I couldn't exactly blame her, or any of them, for looking as ill as they did. It takes time to build up a resistance to that kind of odor. The kind that comes from being exposed to bad food cooked over and over, for years and years.

Polly kept scratching her head. "I can't stand it!" she whispered. "The lice are driving me nuts!"

"Well, be careful," I said. "Don't move around too much. They could spot us. Just don't scratch—"

"I'm trying not to," Polly said, "but Gus—I can't—take—much—more—Aaaaaaaahhhh!" she screamed, rubbing her head harder than she'd ever rubbed it before.

"There they are!" Nurse Gillette shrieked. "Traitors!" She started charging toward us.

I didn't know what to do! I was trapped behind the serving line! I looked at Principal Dane, running toward me with a scowl on her face that had "suspension" written all over it.

Mr. Starchfield was shaking his head back and forth, as if I'd disappointed him beyond all belief.

The janitor was waving his broom, knocking kids over in their chairs as he came after us.

"Hey! Watch it!" Janie Jones cried as she was pitched onto the tile floor.

I had to think fast. Polly was no help—she was jumping around, scratching her head as if there was no tomorrow.

I scooted down to the lunch special—individual vegetarian pizzas. Now, normally I like veggie pizza. But at Thornhill, it's made with lima beans, peas, spinach, yellow squash, and Brussels sprouts. All at once! And instead of tomato sauce on top, they use watery old ketchup. And then they top it all off by spraying on this layer of fake cheese that's made out of one hundred percent oil.

Needless to say, there were a couple hundred left in the serving pan.

I looked at Nurse Gillette coming toward me as if she'd been shot out of a cannon. Then I looked at the pan full of pizzas.

Was I a genius or what?

I picked up a pizza and flung it at her, like a Frisbee.

Her mouth opened in shock—and the pizza hit her right in the face!

CHAPTER FOURTEEN

"Food fight!" somebody screamed.

"Direct hit!" Polly yelled, giving me a high-five. Then she grabbed a couple of pizzas and started hurling them one by one at Nurse Gillette.

A Brussels sprout was hanging out of Nurse Gillette's nose, and she had lima beans on her lips. "Phhhpt," she sputtered, just before Polly's pizzas plastered her hair, knocking off her nurse's cap.

"Gus! Stop! When you fight peace, you create war!" Mr. Starchfield yelled at me.

I reeled off three or four pizzas in his direction.

He hit the floor, as if he was preparing for combat. "Ow!" he cried. "My back's gone out again!"

Two down, three to go! I thought excitedly.

This was a lot more fun than any science fair! If the school got into sponsoring food fights, I'd be sure to win those, too.

Within seconds, everyone in the cafeteria was throwing food at everyone else. Mashed potatoes sailed through the air like rain-filled clouds, only they were filled with brownish-gray gravy—that drenched on contact! Green beans were fired like missiles. Pizzas whizzed past my ear as fast as flying saucers! It was utter mayhem!

The only thing that wouldn't fly was the meat loaf. Every time someone tried to throw a piece, it landed on the floor with a thud. That stuff was about as heavy as a brick. The only person who could throw it was Brad Buggles, who does shot put on the track team.

I laughed out loud as a pizza landed on my head—and stuck! Mashed potatoes dribbled from my ears, and a green bean went down the front of my shirt.

"Quit it!" Polly shrieked as Ray put a pizza cheese-side-down on her head.

"Come on, Polly—your hair's even greasier than this pizza!" he chuckled. "And that's greasy!" He coated her cheek with fake cheese and put mashed potatoes on the end of her nose. "Hey, look, everyone! Polly's ready for Halloween!"

He was still laughing when the pizza I threw hit him on the back of the neck. He dropped to the ground in a pathetic heap.

"So there, Roach!" I cried.

Suddenly, the sound of an ear-piercing whistle came from up above me. I looked up.

Coach K. was standing on a table, with a giant whistle in his mouth. "Stop this right now!" he commanded. "Or gym class will increase from one hour to two hours!"

Everyone started throwing things even harder.

"Correction!" Coach K. yelled. "Stop this right now or gym class will be canceled altogether and you'll have to stay in the cafeteria for recess!"

Instant silence.

"Now, Principal Dane, is there something you'd like to say?" Coach K. asked.

"Yes," she said, pushing her gravy-soaked hair out of her face. "I know who's responsible for this, and I want to see both Gus Moulder and Polly Petri in a minute. Don't go anywhere," she said, with a stern look at both of us.

I gulped. Uh-oh.

"However, given the condition of the rest of the students...not to mention the teachers"—she glanced around the cafeteria—"I have no choice but to cancel school for the rest of the day. I instruct everyone to go home and get cleaned up immediately!"

Everyone cheered.

"Yeah, Gus! Yeah, Polly! Oh, gosh," *clap-clap*,

"Oh, golly," *clap-clap*, "it's time to thank," *clap-clap*, "Gus and Polly!" the cheerleading squad chanted.

Man, those girls can think fast on their feet.

I started running for the door, hoping I could escape with the crush of students heading outside.

Coach K. stepped in front of me. "Going somewhere, Moulder?"

"Oh, uh, no," I said.

"You know, I saw you throw that pizza at Nurse Gillette," he said under his breath. "I think you've got just as good an arm as your brother, after all."

"Thank you, sir," I said, smiling proudly.

"Not that it's going to get you out of this mess!" he added, then he walked off, chuckling to himself.

I frowned, waiting for Principal Dane. Before long, all the students had left, except me and Polly. The janitor had helped Lucille up and was going to drive her home. But we were surrounded by adults: Principal Dane, Mr. Starchfield, and Nurse Gillette. They were all staring intensely at us.

"Gus? Polly? Do you have anything to say?" Principal Dane asked.

Polly nodded eagerly. "We only ran away because of Nurse Gillette. She started the whole thing! We were only trying to save ourselves!"

111

She burst into tears. I could tell she was faking it, because I'd heard her cry for real before, at Dr. Dreck's. But they couldn't tell. And her sad routine was really working!

"What do you mean, dear?" Principal Dane asked. "What did Nurse Gillette do?"

"I—she—" Polly burst out crying again. "Ask Gus!"

Man, she was good!

"Gus? Was there some sort of problem?" the principal asked.

"The last thing I knew, they were leaving my class because they had developed head lice," Mr. Starchfield said.

"Head lice!" Principal Dane exclaimed. "Horrors!"

"They may well have gone to see the nurse," Mr. Starchfield went on. "I mean, their story checks out, so far."

"We did go to see her," I said slowly. "We thought she could help us. But all she wanted to do was shave our heads! And I'm no doctor, but I knew a kid with lice once, and he sure didn't have to get *his* head shaved—"

"Well, no. That's not standard medical procedure," the principal said. "Isn't that a bit unusual, Nurse Gillette?"

"Unusual, but effective!" Nurse Gillette claimed.

"And how exactly did you arrive at this conclusion?" Mr. Starchfield asked.

"Because...it works?! I mean, you've got to get rid of the lice, which are in the hair, so if you get rid of the hair—" Nurse Gillette started to argue.

"If my hair is gone, my life is over!" Polly cried. "Don't you understand anything?"

"You can't go around shaving kids' heads just because you *think* it'll work!" Principal Dane said.

Principal Dane shook her head. "You're a failure as a nurse, Ms. Gillette! I won't even call you Nurse Gillette anymore. And do you know why?" she said, reaching for Nurse Gillette's cap.

"Um..."

"Because you're fired! Clear out your office by two o'clock!" the principal said. She took off Nurse Gillette's cap and tossed it to the floor. "You're history!"

Mr. Starchfield nodded. "Yeah! What she said!" He punched his fist in the air.

Then, when he saw us staring at him, he blushed. "I mean, uh, sometimes the only way to resolve *conflict* is to, uh, *inflict* resolution."

Nurse Gillette stuck her nose in the air and marched toward the door. Before she left, she turned around and said, "I'll be back someday. When you least expect it!"

"She sounds like the Terminator," Polly said, giggling.

"More like the Germinator," I said, laughing.

Principal Dane cleared her throat. "Now, I'm sorry you had to go through that, but I'm afraid you're not totally innocent. You're the ones who started this food fight." She indicated the messy, trashed cafeteria. "And that means you're the ones who are going to have to clean it up."

Polly groaned. "The whole thing? But we'll be here for hours! I want to go home and take a shower!"

"Look at it this way," Principal Dane said. "The faster you clean, the faster you'll be out of here. The mops are right in there." She pointed to a door marked HAZARDOUS WASTE DISPOSAL.

I sighed, walking over to it. "We might as well get started."

We'd been cleaning for over two hours when Polly sank into one of the few non-gravy-slimed chairs. "I can't mop anymore," she said. "You'll have to go on without me." She yawned, stretching her arms over her head.

"I don't know about that," I said with a frown, stopping to lean on my mop. I felt as if all I was doing was smearing gravy in between the cracks in the tile floor. I was collecting a stack of pizzas under one table, and there was a pile of meat loaf that looked like...well, never mind.

"You know what, Gus? Ever since the food fight...I don't think I've scratched my head once," Polly said. "Maybe I've just been too busy. But it doesn't itch at all!"

"Hey, now that you mention it..." I said slowly. "I haven't, either!"

"You know what I think? It's all the cafeteria food in our hair. It killed the lice!"

"But—that's ridiculous!" I cried.

Polly got out of her chair and walked toward me. "Is it? Is it really so ridiculous, Gus?"

"I don't know!" I said. "I'm asking you, remember?"

"Well, why not? If it's strong enough to make us sick...maybe it also has the power to make us well!" Polly said. "Obviously it has some special chemical properties. Maybe we'll never understand how or why...but let's face it, those lice are history!"

"Wow," I breathed. "You're brilliant," I told Polly.

"Wrong," she said. "I'm brilliant *and* beautiful."

"Just like me," I said, smiling.

"Yeah." She nodded. "Right. What*ever!* I'm going home to take a shower, and then it's hello, social life!" Then she tossed her slimy brown hair over her shoulder and walked out of the cafeteria.

I just smiled, holding on to my mop. The real

Polly Petri was back! Not only that, but I had an idea for my science fair project: the effect of Thornhill Middle School cafeteria food on living things. Theory: it killed them all!

I started dancing around the cafeteria with the mop. I didn't even care that Polly had left me to finish cleaning up. I couldn't have been happier!

Unless of course they'd kicked Ray out of school at the same time that they fired Nurse Gillette.

But that was asking for too much. No, I'd just have to beat him in the science fair and enjoy having him as my personal servant.

CHAPTER FIFTEEN

"Hey, Polly! Did you hear about my new project for the science fair?" I asked as I walked into class the next morning. I had finally showered and was wearing normal shoes.

Polly was surrounded by her friends on the cheerleading team, and they were all talking a mile a minute. She turned to me slowly, as if she was forcing herself to be nice. "Uh...no," she said. "How would I hear about it, unless I was absolutely desperate for some really boring information?"

"Yeah, yeah," I said, knowing she was only trying to show off in front of the squad. "Anyway. Check this out. I'm doing a study on the cafeteria food. I mean, if it can kill head lice," I whispered so her friends wouldn't overhear, "imagine what it can do to ants. And spiders! And—"

"Thrillsville," she said, pretending to yawn by

delicately patting her mouth. "Do you mind if I get back to my *own* conversation now?"

I grinned and shook my head. The old Polly Petri was back!

I went over to my seat in front of Ray. He was crunching his barbecued chips, as usual, but he didn't look happy about it. Maybe it was a stale batch.

"Hey, Ray," I said. "You stole my science experiment, but I'm going to win anyway! I've got a totally new project," I announced.

"Yeah?" Ray asked with a sigh. "You probably will win."

I almost fell over. "What do you mean? Since when do you give up so easily?"

"Since...last night. I...I think I killed your tongue fungus," Ray admitted, looking sheepish for the first time.

"You killed *Moldus Maximus?*" I asked, stunned. "How?"

"Well, I don't know...I guess it was the barbecued chips I left on it," Ray said.

"You covered a prize fungus with *chips?*" I asked. "Why would you do that?"

"I thought he—I mean, it—might be hungry," Ray said.

"Hungry?" I sputtered. "Hungry? You think molds like to eat?"

Ray shrugged. "They don't?"

"They're not mammals, you idiot," I said.

"I know that!" Ray said. "They're...reptiles, right?"

"No! Not even close!" I shouted.

"Oh. Well, I don't know what happened, really," Ray said. "I mean, I don't know whether it was the chips that killed it, or the slugs that ate it. I found one chomping on the remains this morning. I mean, I don't know how to do an autopsy on a fungus. But if you want the body..."

"What did you think I was going to do—have a funeral?" I asked.

"Well, you guys were friends, right?" Ray asked.

"I'm a scientist, Ray. I'm objective," I said. "I don't get involved."

But when I sat down at my desk and faced forward, I felt a little tear roll down my cheek. *Moldus Maximus* was dead!

I'd never forgive Ray. Never!

That night after dinner, I went out to the garage and stared at all the dead and dying fungi and molds on my shelves. First Ray was killing my prize fungus, now Jake was doing away with the rest....

Well, I didn't have to just *take* it, did I?

Jake's dumb boat of a car was parked in the garage, taking a break from spewing fumes on my molds. Mr. Hot Shot was inside the house, getting ready for his big Friday night date with

Gloria, our neighbor from down the block. He'd been asking her out for a year, and she'd finally said yes.

I started picking up all the fungi I'd collected. I quickly opened the front door of Jake's car and tossed everything onto the front seat. I could always get more, I told myself—that's the great thing about fungus. They're everywhere!

Then I ran into the house and quickly grabbed a bag of barbecued chips. I had to hurry—Jake's date was coming over in a couple of minutes. I opened the bag and sprinkled the barbecued chips on top of all the fungus. The car was already starting to smell!

Then I went out to my mom's garden and rooted around for a couple of slugs. I found a handful—one giant yellow one, a few green ones, and a couple of gray slugs, too.

I laid them on top of the fungi and mold on the front seat. I peeked out at the street, and saw Gloria, Jake's date, heading toward our house.

I ran out of the garage and hid behind a bush.

"Gloria! Hi!" Jake said, opening the front door.

"Hi, Jake," she said, smiling.

"Wow, you look great," Jake told her.

"Oh, thanks. I just got this skirt from the mall," she said.

I rubbed my hands together. This was going to be even better than I expected!

"Let's get going. The movie starts in fifteen minutes," Jake said.

"Okay!" she said. "Where's your car?"

"In the garage," Jake said. "I like to keep it protected from the sun and rain and all that stuff."

And he likes to kill fungi with it, too! I thought. But Jake wasn't going to get off that easy.

"Wow," Gloria said when she saw Jake's car. "That's...really cool. And...old."

I was starting to like Gloria.

"Yeah, well. It's only for a little while. When I go to college, I'll get a new car," Jake bragged.

Dream on! I thought.

Gloria was standing beside the car, as if she was waiting for Jake to open the door for her. Only he was so clueless, he didn't notice. He just opened his door and slid into the car.

So Gloria did the same thing.

I looked at my watch. One, two, three—

"Aaaah!" Gloria shrieked. "Aaaah! What is this? What's the big idea?" She flung the door open, and it crashed into the wall.

"Hey—watch it!" Jake said.

"No, you watch it!" Gloria yelled, getting out of the car. "And watch that! And that!" She pointed frantically at the car seat.

"What the—"

"Some date you are! Why don't you go back

to middle school instead of college? You're the most childish, immature—"

"Oh, yeah?" Jake said, getting out of the car. "Well, at least I don't have a slug on my leg!"

Gloria glanced down at her leg and shrieked, plucking it off. Then she turned around and saw the two slugs sticking to the back of her skirt! She'd sat on them and smashed them to death! "Slug guts! Gross!" She started shaking her rear end back and forth, trying to get the slugs to fall off. "How could you do this to me!"

I stood up, pumping my fist in the air. "Yes! The Revenge of the Molds!"

"I heard you, Shrimp!" Jake yelled, running toward me. "I'll get you for this!"

I took the last piece of fungus out of my pocket and threw it onto the ground in front of me. He stepped on it—and his feet went out from underneath him! "Aaaah!" he yelled, landing on his butt.

I stood up and pumped my fist in the air.

The Revenge of the Molds was complete!

Gross yourself out and
catch Nurse Gillette's
revenge in

SLIMEBALLS #2

FUN GUS SLIMES THE BUS!

I was getting dressed when I heard this loud booming honk coming from the street. I lifted the blinds and looked out the window. It was the school bus!

What was it doing here already? It wasn't supposed to come for another half-hour!

I pulled on my blue jeans and sneakers and flew down the stairs, grabbing my lunch and books on the way out the door.

"Guuuuus! Breakfast!" my mother yelled.

"No time!" I shouted, skidding around the corner at the bottom of the stairs. I raced across our yard and stepped onto the bus.

"How come you're so early, Mr. Donnelley?" I asked.

"I'm not Mr. Donnelley," a woman's voice replied.

I stared at the bus driver. She sounded familiar, but with that big cap on her head, I couldn't see who she was.

"Well...what happened to Mr. Donnelley, then?" I asked.

"He got sick," she replied. "He won't be back. Now step behind the white line, young man, and take your seat so I can get back on the road. We're falling behind schedule!"

I gulped. It couldn't be.

Then she pushed her cap back on her forehead. "*Today*, Augustus?"

It was Nurse Gillette! Or ex-Nurse Gillette! The woman who'd tried to shave my head and dunked my feet in a bucket of iodine! The woman who got fired because of me—and Polly Petri!

I had to get off the bus right away!

I was about to run for my life, when Nurse Gillette yanked the door closed behind me.

"I—I forgot something," I stammered. "I—"

"Sit down," she barked. "I can't fall behind schedule on my first day!"

"But you're ahead of schedule," I said. "By a whole half an hour!"

"I have my own schedule," she said firmly. "Forget Mr. Donnelley! He was a slacker! We've got a new routine now!" She revved the engine, and I noticed she was wearing shiny new bus driver's platform shoes. "Now take a seat!"

"G-gladly," I sputtered, walking down the

aisle. Everyone was sitting there, chatting and laughing—as if we weren't being driven to school by a total maniac! Of course, *they* hadn't gotten her fired. They were probably safe!

I made my way to the back of the bus, looking for Polly. If anyone would understand how scared I felt, it was her. At first I couldn't find her anywhere. She'd probably seen Nurse Gillette driving and refused to get on the bus!

But then I saw her. And when I did, I almost wished I hadn't!

She was sitting with Ray Roches—the total creep of the universe—and she was holding his hand!

I rushed to the seat in front of them and opened the window, trying to get some fresh air. I felt like I was going to puke!

"Do not open the windows," Nurse Gillette's voice boomed over the speakers in the back of the bus. "It's against the law."

"Since when?" I asked.

"Since I took over this route. Safety first!" Nurse Gillette said. "Besides, I don't want anything to interfere with my air freshening system!"

I glanced at the roof of the bus. A million little pink car fresheners in the shape of pine trees were hanging down, like a mobile. And they stank like artificial strawberry!

"Polly!" I said desperately, turning around. "Polly!"

She was staring at Ray as if he was a movie star or something. I just couldn't understand it. Ray was the rudest, most disgusting kid in our entire class. What was wrong with her?

"Yeah?" she said lazily.

"Polly, did you see who's driving the bus?" I asked.

She shrugged. "Not really. Why?"

"It's Nurse Gillette," I told her.

"Oh," she said.

"Oh!" I repeated. "Is that all you can say?"

"Moulder, we're busy," Ray said gruffly. "Leave us alone."

"You're busy? Doing what?" I asked.

"We're in love, okay?" Ray said.

"Polly?" I gasped. "Is that true? No—don't answer that." I was having a hard enough time not getting sick with all those strawberry pine trees hanging all over my shoulders. "Look, Nurse Gillette is driving the bus, you guys! She tried to kill us once before, Polly—"

"She was only trying to help," Polly said dreamily, still staring into Ray's eyes.

"To help!" I said. "She wanted to turn our heads into bowling balls! And if it weren't for us, she'd still be the school nurse. Do you think she's forgotten that?" I said. "We shouldn't even be on her bus!"

"Well, whatever," Polly said. "I'm sure it'll work out. And if it doesn't, I know Ray will save me. Won't you, Ray-Gun?"

"Definitely, Polly-Wolly," Ray said, leaning forward to kiss Polly—on the lips!

Kissing! Cute nicknames! Polly and Ray? Just thinking about it made my head feel as if it was going to explode. I shook my head and pinched my arm, trying to wake up from the nightmare. But it was no nightmare! It was really happening!

I held on to the seat as the bus rounded a corner at top speed.

"Hey!" Janie Jones yelled, landing on the floor with a thud. "Watch it!"

"Hang on, kids! I've got to make up for lost time!" Nurse Gillette said over the speaker. "It's going to be a bumpy ride!" Then she floored it, and the bus roared ahead, the wheels crashing onto a dirt road covered with rocks.

"This isn't the right way!" I yelled. "Where are you going?"

"It's a shortcut I know!" Nurse Gillette said. "Trust me—we'll get there faster!" The bus pitched to one side as we ran over a small boulder. Nurse Gillette swerved and lunged onto a field, just missing a cow.

I had a feeling I was in for the ride of my life!